What's Bugging Bailey Blecker?

WHAT'S BUGGING

Bailey Blecker?

GAIL DONOVAN

DUTTON CHILDREN'S BOOKS
An imprint of Penguin Group (USA) Inc.

DUTTON CHILDREN'S BOOKS
A division of Penguin Young Readers Group

Published by the Penguin Group
Penguin Group (USA) Inc., 375 Hudson Street, New York, New York 10014, U.S.A.
Penguin Group (Canada), 90 Eglinton Avenue East, Suite 700, Toronto, Ontario M4P 2Y3, Canada
(a division of Pearson Penguin Canada Inc.)
Penguin Books Ltd, 80 Strand, London WC2R 0RL, England
Penguin Ireland, 25 St Stephen's Green, Dublin 2, Ireland (a division of Penguin Books Ltd)
Penguin Group (Australia), 250 Camberwell Road, Camberwell, Victoria 3124, Australia
(a division of Pearson Australia Group Pty Ltd)
Penguin Books India Pvt Ltd, 11 Community Centre, Panchsheel Park, New Delhi—110 017, India
Penguin Group (NZ), 67 Apollo Drive, Rosedale, North Shore 0632, New Zealand
(a division of Pearson New Zealand Ltd)
Penguin Books (South Africa) (Pty) Ltd, 24 Sturdee Avenue, Rosebank, Johannesburg 2196, South Africa
Penguin Books Ltd, Registered Offices: 80 Strand, London WC2R 0RL, England

Library of Congress Cataloging-in-Publication Data

Donovan, Gail, date.
What's bugging Bailey Blecker? / by Gail Donovan.—1st ed.
p. cm.
Summary: When fifth-grader Bailey, who lives on an island off the coast of Maine,
suffers a series of setbacks, including a lice outbreak at school,
it will take every ounce of her determination and the help of
new school friends to get everything back together.
ISBN 978-0-525-42286-0 (hardcover)
[1. Islands—Fiction. 2. Maine—Fiction. 3. Schools—Fiction. 4.
Lice—Fiction.] I. Title. II. Title: What is bugging Bailey Blecker?
PZ7.D7227Wh 2011
[Fic]—dc22   2010013308

Published in the United States by Dutton Children's Books,
a division of Penguin Young Readers Group
345 Hudson Street, New York, New York 10014
www.penguin.com/youngreaders

Designed by *Irene Vandervoort*

Printed in USA   First Edition

10 9 8 7 6 5 4 3 2 1

For my mother

● ● ● ● ● ●

With thanks to: *Ann Harleman, Lydia-Rose Kesich,*

Zora Kesich, Ihila Lesnikova, Frances Lefkowitz,

and Elizabeth Searle.

Life Cycle of the Head Louse

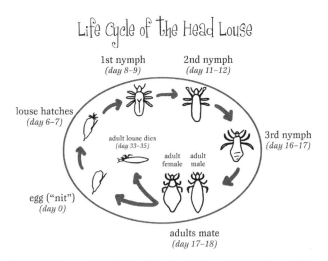

1st nymph
(day 8–9)

2nd nymph
(day 11–12)

louse hatches
(day 6–7)

adult louse dies
(day 33–35)

3rd nymph
(day 16–17)

adult   adult
female   male

egg ("nit")
(day 0)

adults mate
(day 17–18)

Note: Female lays eggs at 18–19 days. She can lay 4–8 eggs each day for the next 16 days.

Contents

What's Bugging Bailey Blecker?

CHAPTER 1

Uninvited Guests

Bailey felt like her arm was going to fall off. She waved her hand. No response.

She switched arms, but after a while her other arm got tired, too. So she braced herself on her desk and propped up her arm with her hand.

Still nothing. Mr. McGovern kept ignoring Bailey, and Bailey kept on ignoring him ignoring her. Because she did not like giving up. Which Bailey called normal and her mother called determined (when she was in a good mood) or just plain stubborn (when she was in a bad mood). When Mr. McGovern was having a good day, he called her persistent. On a bad day, he just didn't call on her at all. Like right now.

Right now Mr. McGovern was reading the poem about the midnight ride of Paul Revere to kick off their unit on the American Revolution, which every kid in the state had to study in fifth grade. The poem started off by saying that the ride happened on the eighteenth of April, a long time ago. And all Bailey wanted to say was that April eighteenth was a holiday called Patriots' Day, but more importantly, it was her birthday. She was ten going on eleven. The point about Patriots' Day was definitely what Mr. McGovern would call "on topic," and even though her birthday was maybe a little bit "off topic," it would only take a second to say. *If* Mr. M. would ever call on her.

Which he still wasn't doing. He paused just long enough to say, "I am not calling on *anyone* right now, fifth graders. I am reading a *poem*."

Bailey knew that *fifth graders* meant her. He meant she should put her hand down.

4

Uninvited Guests

She kept her hand up and Mr. McGovern kept reading.

"One, if by land, and two, if by sea;

And I on the opposite shore will be,

Ready to ride and spread the alarm . . ."

Bailey knew that she had probably gone past determined and past persistent and into "just plain stubborn," but she didn't care. Her arm did care, though. She switched hands again. Problem solved.

Except she had another problem that wasn't so easy to fix: her neck. It itched like crazy. But she couldn't scratch because one hand was raised and the other hand was holding up the tired arm. She couldn't scratch unless she gave up. Which she was *not* going to do.

Mr. McGovern was not giving up, either. He gave her his I'm-the-teacher look, which she ignored by looking out the window. Outside, two landscape guys were spreading mulch around a tree. The smell of wood chips floated through the open window into the classroom, where Mr. McGovern was going on with the poem. And on, and on.

"Meanwhile, impatient to mount and ride,

Booted and spurred, with a heavy stride

On the opposite shore walked Paul Revere . . ."

It seemed like the poem would never end. Bailey didn't think she could take the itchiness much longer. She was going to go crazy if she couldn't scratch. She wondered if a person could die from itchiness.

Bailey didn't want to die. So she let down her hand to scratch the back of her neck. She scratched and scratched. After that, she didn't bother raising either hand again. She needed both for scratching.

Mr. McGovern finally finished reading the poem, closed the book, and looked straight at Bailey.

Mr. M. was one of those teachers who tried to say everything in a positive way. Instead of saying, "No running in the halls! No shouting!" he would say, "We're walking and talking, now. Walk and talk, please." Instead of saying, "This is wrong," he would say, "You don't have this quite right, yet. You need to *stretch* your thinking." Whenever he was thinking up positive things to say, he filled his cheeks full of air and let out a long, slow thinking breath.

He took a deep breath now and said, "Thank you for waiting so patiently, Bailey. Is there something you wanted to share?"

Bailey stopped scratching long enough to say, "April eighteenth is my birthday." Then she had to start scratching again.

Everybody started talking at once, partly because they couldn't take being quiet any longer, and partly because a birthday was good news. Birthdays meant cupcakes during snack.

Bailey's mom had said she had two choices. She could do the best friend sleepover, as usual. Or maybe this year she'd like to ask all her new friends to a big party? That was a no-brainer. No matter what her mom called them, the kids in her new school weren't really friends. She was picking the sleepover with

Olivia, for sure. All she had to do now was make sure Olivia remembered it was this weekend. It was kind of strange—having to make sure, now that they didn't see each other every day at school.

"Fifth graders," said Mr. McGovern as he started passing out their Writer's Notebooks. "We are not having a birthday now. Now we're focusing on Paul Revere's ride. I'd like everybody to write a 'quick response' to the poem. Except you, Bailey. I'd like to talk with you in the hall, please."

Was she in trouble? For being stubborn? Was he mad because she had kept her hand up for practically the entire poem?

"Bailey," he said when they were alone in the hallway. "I'm sending you down to the office."

"Why?" she asked. "How come?"

He took a big positive-thinking breath and held it for a long time, like he couldn't think of any way to be positive about what was coming next. "Just go to the office. I'll call and let them know you're coming. They'll explain down there."

This was weird. Bailey couldn't tell if she was in trouble or not. Just in case she was, she walked as slowly as possible, checking out all the artwork on the walls, and carefully matching her steps to the footprints on the floor.

The footprints were part of this year's schoolwide theme: *Walking in Your Buddy's Shoes*. The whole school was supposed to be working on being empathetic. As a reminder, every classroom had a pair of shoes glued to a piece of poster board, and all the hallway floors had been painted with footprints.

The artwork lining the hallway walls was from their *My Many Moods* unit team-taught by the art teacher and the social worker. There were sad faces and happy faces and angry faces. One kid had drawn a surprised face with the mouth in a big *O*.

Surprises were good. Maybe she wasn't being sent

to the office for something bad. Maybe she was being sent for something good. Maybe she was going to get an award! An award would be good! Bailey picked up the pace—she had to leap over some of the painted footprints—and when she got to the stairs she sprinted down two steps at a time, and ran into the office.

"I'm here!"

The school secretary looked up from her desk and the look on her face did not say *Time for Bailey Blecker to get an award.* It was more of a How-many-years-until-retirement? look.

"Go right in, Bailey," she said, pointing to a door with a glass window. "The nurse is expecting you."

The nurse? Bailey didn't know the nurse, but she did know that seeing the nurse did not qualify as a good surprise. She didn't have time to ask any questions, though, because the nurse had already opened the door and was motioning Bailey inside.

The nurse's room—more like a big closet, really—smelled like Band-Aids. The walls were decorated with posters about coughing into the crook of your arm and washing your hands for as long as it took to sing "Happy Birthday."

"I'm Mrs. Walsh," said the nurse. She was wearing one of those hospital smocks dotted with teddy bears holding balloons. "I don't think we've met, have we?"

Bailey's neck still itched. Scratching, she shook her head. "It's my first year here," she explained. "I went to Fox Island Elementary for kindergarten through fourth. But there were so few fifth graders this year that we had a choice of staying there in a combined four/five class or coming to the mainland school. So I came here."

The nurse made the sort of cooing noise that people always made when they found out she lived on Fox Island. "Oh!" she gushed. "You live on an *island*! That must be *awesome*."

Bailey's hand went up to her neck again to scratch. "It's good," she said.

Bailey was used to the nurse's reaction. She liked

where she lived, on an island off the coast of Maine, but she'd lived there her whole life, so it wasn't a big deal. She lived in a house with her mom. She had a pet bird named Apollo. Except for the fact that she got to school on a ferryboat, it was pretty normal.

What wasn't normal was sitting and chatting with the school nurse. Bailey had figured out that the nurse wasn't handing out any awards. But she still couldn't figure out what she was doing here.

Mrs. Walsh smiled a huge smile, like the grinning teddy bears on her smock. "Gosh!" she said. "You have such long hair! It's down to your waist! And such a pretty color! It's like a brand-new copper penny."

Bailey nodded. She'd gotten used to this, too. People oohing and aahing over her *beautiful* hair.

"I'm going to donate it to *Care Through Hair*," she explained. "You know, for people who are so sick they lost their hair?"

"What a generous thing to do! How long have you been growing it?"

Bailey wasn't exactly sure when she'd started. "A long time," she said, scratching some more. "Like . . . more than a year."

The nurse opened her mouth and closed it, as if she was going to say something, but changed her mind. Then she opened a desk drawer and took out what looked like an extralong chopstick, but with a pointier end.

"Bailey, I'm going to take a look at your head. Maybe I can see why you're so itchy, okay?"

Bailey shrugged. "Okay," she said.

The nurse came around behind Bailey and ran the wooden stick down the back of Bailey's head, like her mom did when she was parting Bailey's hair to put it in two braids.

What Bailey hadn't told the nurse about her hair—because sometimes when she talked about it she felt like she might cry, and crying at school was *not* something she wanted to do—was the reason she was donating it to *Care Through Hair*. The reason was Aunt Jess. Aunt

Jess was Bailey's mom's sister, who was sick. She was going to get better, but the medicines she had to take were going to make her lose all her hair. She was the one who had given Apollo to Bailey, as a present for her last birthday.

The nurse kept parting Bailey's hair in different places and making little noises. They weren't you-live-on-an-island coos, though. They were more like the grumbling noises her mom made when she saw how messy Bailey's room was. They were not happy noises.

"Well, Bailey," said the nurse finally. "It looks like some uninvited guests are visiting you."

She tossed the pointer stick in the trash can. "Sweetheart—I'm afraid you have lice."

· · · · · · · · · · · · ·

CHAPTER 2

Brain Freeze

Bailey felt a chill clench her brain, like the worst ice-cream headache ever.

"Lice?" she shrieked. "Like *bugs*?"

"Insects," said the nurse. "Yes."

"Bugs," repeated Bailey. "On my *head*?"

"They're head lice, so they're only on your head," said the nurse, as if this was good news.

"Bugs—on my head—crawling around?"

"Well, yes, they do crawl," said the nurse, and added—as if this was more good news—"but they can't fly or hop."

Then the nurse proceeded to give Bailey way too much information about lice.

Apparently lice were going around the school. That's why Mr. McGovern had known to send her down to the office, because scratching was one of the telltale signs. But Bailey shouldn't be worried. Lice weren't dangerous; they were only a nuisance. And she should know that it had nothing to do with being dirty. Anyone could get lice, the same way anyone could catch a cold. The nurse would give Bailey's mom a call to let her know, and a schoolwide flyer about the situation would be going home with all the kids today.

Bailey's head was still in a brain freeze. An itchy brain freeze. But it wasn't so frozen that she couldn't figure out why the nurse had been asking all those questions about her hair!

"I don't have to cut my hair, do I?"

"You certainly don't *have* to," said the nurse, "because lice don't live in the long part. They stay right on your scalp, where it's warm. But I have to tell you that there's a lot of shampooing and combing and searching for lice eggs, and the longer your hair, the bigger a job that will be." She gave Bailey a big teddy bear grin and added, "Lice can be awfully stubborn."

Not more stubborn than she was!

Mrs. Walsh stood and ushered Bailey from her office, and the school secretary told Bailey that she should go join her class in the library.

Brain still frozen, Bailey wandered into the library, where kids were roaming through the stacks and Mr. McGovern was saying, "Remember, we're choosing something *appropriate* for Quiet Reading."

Bailey grabbed the first book off the shelf, hurried over to the reading nook, and settled into a beanbag, holding the book in front of her face as if she were reading. She wasn't reading—she just wanted to make sure nobody talked to her. Because she didn't want to talk. Not with anybody *here*, anyway. She wished Olivia were here.

She and Olivia had been best friends ever since

kindergarten at Fox Island Elementary. Then last summer Bailey's mom and Olivia's parents had "explored the option" of the kids switching to Casco Elementary on the mainland. All the island kids came for middle school in sixth grade, but the school district let students come earlier if they wanted. The grown-ups talked about things like a "small and safe learning environment" vs. "the greater resources of a larger school." Bailey knew what that meant. Fifth grade in the island school would be Olivia (good) and the same three boys she'd known *forever* (not so good). Fifth grade in the city would mean an actual band and an actual art room instead of a rolling cart, for starters. It meant something new and different, not the same old thing.

Bailey and her mom and Olivia and her parents decided to go for it. Bailey was scared, but she was psyched, too. She and Olivia were going to do what the big kids did, only they were going to do it first. And they'd do it together.

Until Olivia's parents changed their minds, right before school started. And Olivia didn't argue. She chickened out! She wanted to stay on the island. But Bailey didn't want to stay. She'd made up her mind to go, and she didn't want to change it back. Which was how they'd ended up in different schools this year. The kids here at Casco had been nice enough to her, but they already *had* their best friends. Bailey was the new kid, all by herself.

She and Olivia were still best friends—sort of. But it wasn't the same, not being in school together. Next year they'd both be in the mainland middle school, and ride the ferry together, and Bailey was positive that they'd go back to being *real* best friends again. But right now she didn't exactly have a best friend.

What she had right now was lice.

She squeezed her eyes shut, trying not to think about the lice. Bugs. On her head. Crawling around.

"Hide me," said a voice.

Bailey opened her eyes.

19

It was Lexy. "Hide me," she said again. "Here comes Tucker."

Bailey didn't know which kid she'd rather avoid more—Tucker Pierce or Alexis Nguyen. Perfect-attendance Lexy was a know-it-all. And Tucker reminded Bailey of something she didn't want to think about right now: bugs. He was crazy about insects, so every time he got a present it was something with a bug on it. He must have a giant family, Bailey figured, because practically every article of clothing he owned had a bug-related design. Today's shirt had a picture of a scorpion.

Bailey put her book in front of her face again, but that didn't stop either Lexy or Tucker from invading the reading nook.

Tucker pulled an encyclopedia off a shelf. "Will Mr. M. say this is appropriate? It's all about the letter *H*, and right here in Human Anatomy there's a picture—"

"Tucker, stuff it!" warned Bailey. "We're not interested!"

"Besides," added Lexy. "You're supposed to get something you can check out."

"So?" asked Tucker.

"So that's a *reference* book," said Lexy.

Even though Bailey didn't want to see any pictures of male anatomy, she took pity on Tucker. "Encyclopedias have to stay in the library," she explained. "Remember that unit we did on Using Your Resources?"

"I know that," said Tucker. "I'm not stupid."

"Could have fooled me," said Lexy.

Bailey sighed. So much for not wanting to talk to anybody.

Next Arianna Fogelman wandered into the reading nook. Arianna was new since winter break— even newer than Bailey—and she was still kind of a mystery. Rumor had it she had passed all her times tests in the third grade at her old school. Nobody knew for sure, though, because Arianna was the kind of kid who never talked unless it was mandatory. She almost always had her head in a book, reading through her purple-rimmed glasses. And for some reason, her head was always in a leopard-print bandanna.

She didn't say anything now—no surprise—just sat down on a beanbag and started reading.

Bailey tried to read, too, but she couldn't concentrate. She looked up at the Favorite Figures from Literature mobile. A cat, a pig, a rabbit, and a mouse dangled from the ceiling, slowly drifting around each other.

"Hey," said Tucker, who apparently couldn't concentrate, either, "how come you had to go to the principal's?"

Bailey was not the kind of kid who got sent to the principal's office. That would be Tucker. "I didn't," she said.

"Come on, what'd you do?" teased Tucker. "Are you in trouble?"

"I am not in trouble," she said, defending herself. And scratching herself.

Lexy asked, "If you're not in trouble, why did you get sent to the principal's?"

How could know-it-all Lexy not know that Tucker was just trying to be annoying? And why did Tucker have to choose right now to be so annoying?

"I am *not* in trouble," insisted Bailey, scratching some more. "I didn't do anything wrong, and I didn't see the principal," she said, and to prove her point, added, "I saw the nurse."

Which she instantly wished she hadn't said.

"The nurse?" Tucker brightened at this interesting twist in the story. "How come?"

"Bet I know," said a voice.

Bailey and Lexy and Tucker all turned in surprise toward Arianna. Arianna, the girl who only spoke when Mr. M. called on her, was voluntarily talking?

Arianna peered at Bailey through her purple glasses. "Is it lice?"

"Lice!" roared Tucker. "You have lice?"

Bailey felt a burst of heat rush to her face, as if she'd just opened an oven door. "Tucker, shut *up*!" she hissed. She turned to Arianna. "How'd you guess?"

Arianna pointed to her bandanna with its leopard-print pattern. "Why do you think I wear this?"

Lexy pulled a book off the shelf and began thumbing through it. "Because you really like jungle prints?" she asked.

Arianna shook her head. "It's so if anybody else has lice, I'm not getting them." She shuddered. "'Cause having lice sucks. No offense."

"Hey, none taken," said Tucker.

"She wasn't talking to *you*," Bailey scolded. "She was talking to *me*."

Bailey was kind of surprised that Arianna was talking at all. This was the longest conversation they had ever had. She asked, "Does that mean you had them?"

"Yup," admitted Arianna. "At my last school practically everybody in my class got lice. And I'm *never* having them again. I hope."

By now the news that Bailey Blecker had lice must

have spread through the entire fifth grade of Casco Elementary, because everyone started trying to squish into the reading nook.

First on the scene was Max. He and Bailey shared a music stand in band. They both played clarinet. "You have lice?" he asked. "For real?"

Bailey didn't want to tell the world she had lice. But she wasn't going to tell a lie, either. "For real," she admitted.

Rashad appeared next. She played in the band, too. Flute. "How do you know?" she asked.

"The nurse said so."

Emma and Rosa squeezed into the reading nook. They were twins who had been homeschooled until this year, and whose mom insisted they had to be in the same class.

"The nurse said you have lice?" squealed Emma.

"Lice?" echoed Rosa, in an even more high-pitched squeal. "Like cooties?"

"No," corrected Lexy, as if she were some kind of expert. She read from the encyclopedia. "They're called *Pediculus humanus capitis*."

David and Eli and Joey jostled and pushed their way forward. They didn't play in the band. They only played with things you could kick, like soccer balls.

"Otherwise known as cooties!" crowed David. "Let me see!"

"You can't see them," objected Eli. "They're miniature."

"Like your brain," said Joey.

"Hey!" said Eli, giving Joey a shove.

"Hey, no pushing," said Emma.

"Yeah, no pushing," echoed Rosa.

More kids started pushing and shoving. It was like everybody wanted to get close, but not too close. Close enough to see Bailey Blecker, but not so close you might get her cooties. They were all gathered in a circle around her. Staring at her. Max. Rashad. Emma and Rosa. David and Eli and Joey. Arianna and Lexy and Tucker and the whole rest of the fifth grade.

Bailey felt like she was pinned to her beanbag, like she was some kind of specimen in a museum: ten-year-old girl with lice. Otherwise known as *Pediculus humanus capitis*. Otherwise known as cooties.

CHAPTER 3

More Bad

"There will be a short blast of the horn," announced the captain.

The horn sounded and the ferry backed out of its berth and began chugging toward Fox Island, across the bay. The sky was blue, but the ocean was blue and gray and green, like it couldn't make up its mind exactly what color to be.

Bailey had made up her mind. She'd already made it up, but now it was absolutely positively *extra* made up. No way was she going to invite everybody to a big party for her birthday, like her mom wanted. Not after today. Not the way most kids had stared and teased and acted so grossed-out.

Mr. McGovern had finally come rushing over to investigate the commotion. Tucker had announced—as if he'd made an important scientific discovery—that she had lice. Mr. M. drew one of his big breaths, and Bailey wondered how he could possibly put a positive spin on bugs crawling around on her head.

He couldn't. They had checked out their books and gone back to their classroom. The rest of the day was a blur to Bailey. At the end of it Mr. McGovern passed out pieces of neon pink paper that said, *We Have Critters in Our Class!*

On the boat, a seagull flapped by, squawking and staring at her with its yellow eyes. It was windy on the upper deck, but Bailey didn't mind. She liked the salty smell of the air, and the cool breeze felt good on her hot, itchy neck. And it felt good to watch the mainland get smaller and smaller as the island got bigger and bigger.

Fifteen minutes later, the ferry docked. Bailey hefted her backpack onto her shoulders and joined the crowd of people shuffling off the boat and onto the island. Time to go to Zach's house.

Switching schools wasn't the only plan that Bailey and Olivia had made last summer. They had the teaming-up-on-babysitting idea, too. They knew that Zach's mom, Lucy Sawyer, needed a mother's helper in the afternoons, after Zach woke up from his afternoon nap and before Mr. Sawyer got home from work. Mrs. Sawyer agreed to hire them as a team, with Bailey and Olivia splitting the afternoons between them. Except then it turned out they were in different schools, and working on different afternoons, which meant Bailey didn't see Olivia during school or after school, either. Which wasn't how she planned it.

Bailey might need to go straight to Zach's today, but that didn't mean she had to go in a straight line to get there. After passing the stores that clustered near the wharf—the Snack Shack and Island Groceries and

More Bad

Bob's Bike Repair & Rentals—she zigged and zagged along the dirt roads that crisscrossed the island. That was one of the cool things about living on an island: the roaming. Parents let their kids wander pretty much where they wanted. They knew there were two reasons the kids could never get lost.

The first reason was because no matter where you were, if you walked long enough you'd come to one of the four biggies: Big Loop, Little Loop, Wharf Street, or Beach Road. The four biggies did just what their names said. Big Loop ran around the perimeter of the island. Inside that, Little Loop made a smaller circle. Wharf Street led to the wharf—or away from it, depending on where you were going. Beach Road led to—or away from—the beach.

The second reason you could never get lost was because every ten feet you ran into somebody who knew you.

"Miss Blecker!" said Mr. Adams, who was standing on the front lawn of the Historical Society, holding a pair of pruners in one hand and a lopped-off tree branch in the other. Today he was wearing a navy blue Windbreaker, but Bailey had seen him dressed like a Revolutionary War soldier when the society staged their reenactments. His curlicue mustache looked better when he was all dressed up. He talked like he was from another century, too.

"Hi, Mr. Adams," said Bailey.

"Tremendous to see you! How are you on this grand April afternoon?"

He swept his arm wide to point out the grandeur of the spring day: blue sky, green grass, patches of yellow daffodils, and big, shaggy bushes of yellow forsythia.

Bailey didn't want to go into how she actually was, so she answered, "Fine. How are you?"

"I," he declared, "am at war." He held up the branch to show her his enemy.

Bailey's stomach made a swooping dive, the way it did when she jumped off the wharf in the summer.

Stuck to the branch was what looked like a big cobweb. Inside the web, too many caterpillars to count were wriggling and writhing around.

"What are they?" she asked.

"Tent caterpillars," said Mr. Adams. "Self-explanatory, I'm afraid. They are caterpillars that make little tents. Very damaging to the trees. And so, before the trees leaf out, I need to eradicate these pests from the branches. I don't suppose you'd like to earn some money by joining in the battle?"

Bailey liked Mr. Adams, even if he was in a time warp, and she liked earning money. But even if she didn't have to get to her babysitting job, there was no way she could deal with any more bugs today. "I would," she said, "but I can't right now."

"Carry on, then," he said, waving her on, then shouting, "Wait!"

Bailey stopped. Mr. Adams was one of those one-more-thing people. You never had a quick talk with Mr. Adams.

"I almost forgot! You'll be participating in our little event this year, won't you?"

Every spring the Historical Society—which was basically Mr. Adams and a few of his cronies—teamed up with the Fox Island Elementary fifth grade to reenact a scene from the American Revolution. Last year they'd staged the signing of the Declaration of Independence. The year before that it was the battle of Lexington and Concord. The teachers liked it because they got to check both history and community service off their to-do list. The kids liked it because Mr. Adams was more fun than their regular teachers.

"I don't think so," admitted Bailey.

The Revolutionary War Reenactment Day was one of the biggest deals of the year for the Fox Island fifth graders. When Bailey was little, she couldn't wait to be in it. But Bailey didn't go to Fox Island Elementary anymore. How could she take part in Reenactment Day when she couldn't be at all the lessons and rehearsals?

Probably she wouldn't be allowed. It wouldn't be fair.

"You know I'm not in the island school this year, right?"

"You're still a fifth grader aren't you?" cried Mr. Adams. "And don't all fifth graders in our great state study the American Revolution?"

Scratching, Bailey nodded. "Yes."

"And wouldn't you like to participate?"

"For sure!" said Bailey. "But will that be okay with the school?"

Mr. Adams made a snorting noise. "I'll speak to the school. I'm the commander of this army, aren't I? Or at least, I've played General Washington before. So that's settled. Marvelous. Off you go."

He bowed and waved her on for real this time, and Bailey ran down the road. April meant that the dirt road was more like a mud road, but Bailey didn't care. She leaped over the squelchiest spots. She had an invitation to Reenactment Day from Mr. Adams!

In a few minutes she reached the Sawyers' house. Mrs. Sawyer was standing outside on the porch, with Zach perched on her hip.

"Bailey," she called out, "I'm so sorry you can't come this afternoon!"

Bailey bounded up the porch steps. "What do you mean? I can come! I'm right here!"

"Your mom called, honey."

"My mom? Called you?"

"She called me after the school called her. To tell her about the—"

Mrs. Sawyer paused and made a face, and suddenly Bailey understood what was happening. She knew what was coming next. It was like when you made a sand castle, and you could see a wave on its way in, getting bigger and bigger as it got closer.

"—the lice," Mrs. Sawyer finally managed.

Crash. That was the wave, freezing cold.

"That's okay!" protested Bailey. "I can still babysit!"

Mrs. Sawyer shook her head. "I'd love to have help,

Bailey. The house is a mess and I was hoping to get some cleaning done." She put Zach down. "But I can't risk it, sweetheart. The last thing I need is me or Zach getting lice."

Zach tottered over toward Bailey. "Bai-ee," he said, lifting his arms. "Up!"

Bailey wanted to pick him up, but she didn't dare. What if a louse crawled from her head onto his? She'd never get a babysitting job again.

Mrs. Sawyer and Zach went back inside, and Bailey went back down the steps, and on down the muddy road.

It was hard to believe what a crazy day this had been so far.

First she found out she had lice. That was bad.

Then she got a Reenactment Day invitation from Mr. Adams. That was good.

Then she lost her mother's helper job. More bad.

Bad—good—more bad—now what? What was coming next on this crazy day?

CHAPTER 4

· · · · · · · · · · · · ·

Tidal Wave

A big fight with her mom was next.

Trudging into the house, Bailey could hear Apollo calling loudly for attention, the way he always did when she came home. She expected that. What she did not expect was to find her mom sitting at the kitchen table. What was her mother doing home from work this early?

Bailey dropped her backpack on the floor. "Mom, what's going on? Why did you call Mrs. Sawyer? Now I'm, like, fired!"

"I called because it was the right thing to do,

honeybee," said Bailey's mom. Bee—or honeybee—was her nickname for Bailey. "And I came home early so we can get started dealing with the"—she paused the same way Mrs. Sawyer had, like it was bad luck just to say the word—"lice."

Bailey's mom was in her usual outfit, jeans and a big button-down shirt. She worked all over the island, doing housecleaning and gardening. She liked to say she helped people make everything "shipshape," inside or out, which Bailey thought was a Mr. M. type of positive spin on weeding and vacuuming.

Some of her mom's positive spins were no big deal. For example, her mom had brown hair with streaks of what she liked to call "silver" instead of gray. No biggie.

But sometimes her mom's upbeat attitude had a way of turning into a downward spiral for Bailey. Like the time her mom had the "great idea" to compost all winter long and ordered a hundred worms, which Bailey was supposed to keep alive in big buckets in the basement. Before that it was Friendship Bread. Her mom kept feeding sourdough starter and making Bailey deliver batches of it to everyone they knew until practically the entire island was drowning in Friendship Bread. Bailey had learned to stay as far away as possible when her mom had a "great idea."

Bailey's mother held out her hand. "May I please see the paper the school sent home? And would you please turn the volume down on that bird so I can think straight?"

Bailey fished the hot pink *We Have Critters in Our Class!* paper from her backpack, gave it to her mom, and went over to quiet down Apollo.

When Aunt Jess first gave her Apollo, he had lived in a small cage. Then Bailey started wondering if he would be happier with more room. Enough room to fly. At first she wanted to get him a bigger cage. But then she learned what an aviary was—a little room, just for birds. She started in on convincing her mom, and after only a few weeks of persistence and determination, her mom said yes.

Bailey and Aunt Jess had spent an entire weekend clearing out the pantry off the kitchen. They took out all the junk that had piled up and took down the shelves. What was left was a small room with a window at one end and an open doorway at the other, which they closed up by hanging a screen door. They had made an aviary.

Bailey slipped in there now, and holding out her hand, said, "Step up!"

That was what her bird book said to do if you were trying to train your bird to come when you called, which she was. She wanted to have Apollo trained by the next time Aunt Jess came out to the island. Bailey didn't know when that would be. Right now Aunt Jess was staying with a friend down in Massachusetts, while she had more treatments. Next time they saw her, she wouldn't have any hair. But maybe—hopefully—she'd be getting better.

"Step up!" repeated Bailey, but Apollo didn't come to her hand. From his perch, he just chirped and tilted his head at her. His head and belly were lemon yellow and his wings were lime green.

"This doesn't tell me much," said Bailey's mom, reading from the *Critters* sheet. "What did the nurse say?"

"She said lice were going around the whole school," said Bailey as she tried again. Holding out her hand, she coaxed, "Step up!"

Nothing. Apollo still wouldn't land on her outstretched hand. The bird book also said to put your bird in a smaller space for training. But should she really take Apollo out of his big, beautiful aviary where the perches were real tree branches? Should she really put him back in his little cage?

"That's all?"

Bailey hesitated. She had a feeling that maybe she shouldn't tell her mom everything the nurse had said. How the longer her hair was, the more work it would be to get rid of the lice.

"She said they're only on my head. Because they're head lice."

Bailey's mom had a way of knowing when Bailey wasn't telling her something. It was like she could sense Bailey hiding a mess, like dirty clothes under the bed.

"I know that," said her mom. "Was there anything else?"

Bailey thought back to the conversation and came up with something else. "She said lice were more like a nuisance than a disease."

Bailey's mom rolled up the sleeves of her big white shirt, like she was getting ready to make things seriously shipshape, and crossed her arms. "Bailey Blecker, what aren't you telling me?"

Bailey slipped out from the aviary. Carefully, she closed the screen door so Apollo couldn't get out. She had to be careful how she answered her mom, too. She decided to go with the quick answer and then a change of subject. "She-said-lice-could-be-really-stubborn-and-that-it-might-take-longer-to-get-rid-of-them-with-long-hair. Where's Apollo's old cage?"

Her mom answered automatically, "Down in the cellar, probably," and Bailey saved herself from any more questions by running down the cellar stairs as fast as she could.

Down in the cellar it was cool and damp and dim, with curtains of cobwebs over the tiny windows. Bailey rummaged through the mounds of junk. An old television. Empty buckets (the failed worm fiasco) and tools they weren't using right now, like snow shovels and rakes for autumn leaves. A lot of the stuff that used to be in the pantry. In a corner, she spotted the cage. And there was a butterfly net in a pile of old toys. She'd need that, too. She grabbed the cage and net, went back up to the kitchen and into the aviary.

"What does that mean?" asked her mom, continuing their conversation as if Bailey had never left. "Was she saying you should cut your hair?"

There was a knock on the door—saved again!

It was almost like Olivia's hair appeared before Olivia did—there was so much of it and it was so bright. Her hair was golden orange, like the color of orange soda, and as frizzy as frizzy got.

"Come on in, Olivia," said Bailey's mom, briefly sidetracked from the hair issue. "We haven't seen you for a while. What have you been up to?"

"Not much," said Olivia as she came in with Miss Jane's dog on a leash. "Just . . . stuff." She turned to Bailey. "I went by the Sawyers' to see if you and Zach wanted to help walk Shackleton, but Mrs. S. said they were taking a day off. So . . . you want to come with?"

Lots of island kids volunteered to walk Shackleton because Miss Jane was getting too old to go out much. Bailey definitely wanted to go with Olivia. They hadn't hung together since—Bailey couldn't exactly remember the last time she and Olivia had hung out.

"For sure!" she said. "In a minute, okay? I gotta get Apollo into this cage."

"Okay," agreed Olivia.

Bailey's mom got back on track. "Bailey, wait," she

said, sounding annoyed. "I asked if the nurse said you should cut your hair?"

Olivia sat down in a kitchen chair and pulled fluffy, white Shackleton up onto her lap. "You're cutting your hair?" she asked. "I love your hair!"

Olivia wanted straight hair, like Bailey's. She hated her own unruly orange hair.

Bailey started trying to catch Apollo with the butterfly net. "I'm not cutting my hair, Mom. All she said was I might want to think about it."

"Well, are you? Because it sounds to me like it might be a good idea."

"Mom," said Bailey, "it is *not* a good idea."

"Bailey Blecker," said her mom, "I hope you're not going to turn this into another one of your exhibitions on just how stubborn you can be."

Bailey made another unsuccessful pass with the butterfly net. She couldn't help being stubborn. That was just the way she was. The only thing that changed was whether her mother approved or disapproved of whatever it was that Bailey was being stubborn *about*.

If her mom approved, then Bailey was praised. Like when Bailey had learned how to read. Apparently she had spent the summer between kindergarten and first grade poring over her favorite picture books, the ones she already knew by heart. By the end of the summer she was reading. Since reading was a good thing, Bailey had been praised as *determined*.

Stubborn was reserved for all the things Bailey was determined about that her mom felt made life difficult.

Age four: only eating food that was white, like pasta, milk, and bread. Age five: wearing—for basically an entire year—the flower girl dress somebody had handed down to her. Age six: insisting on tying her own shoes even though they took half an hour to tie and ten seconds to come untied. And so on.

Bailey frankly felt that all these examples of her stubbornness might have slightly inconvenienced her mother, but that they weren't that big a deal. The way she saw it, she hadn't asked her mom to eat white food or wear flower girl dresses, so what was the problem?

"Bailey," said her mom in a warning voice.

Bailey made another pass with the net and there!—she had him. Quickly she put the net inside the old cage, and released Apollo. Then she came out from the aviary and placed the cage—now holding Apollo—on a stool. His little yellow body was puffing in and out with his heartbeats.

"Bailey!" said her mom again, more loudly.

Bailey knew that nothing was going to save her now. And by now Olivia's orange head was pinging and ponging back and forth as she followed what was definitely turning into an argument between Bailey and her mom. Ping—she looked at Bailey.

"I can't help being stubborn," said Bailey. "That's just the way I am!"

Pong—Olivia looked to Bailey's mom, who said, "What do you mean, *that's just the way I am*? You're ten years old! Your character isn't set in stone. There are times you have to mix it up—go with the flow—and this might be one of them."

Ping. Eyes on Bailey. Who had no intention of going with any flow. It wasn't only *Care Through Hair* and Aunt Jess. It was her hair, which everyone said was so beautiful. If she chopped off all her hair now it would be . . . gone! It would be gone *and* she would have failed to do something special. She'd just be a failure with boring old short hair.

"I'm going to cut my hair," she said, "but not *now*. Don't you know how long I've been growing it?"

Olivia's orange head ponged back toward Bailey's mom.

"Of course I know: ever since Jess was diagnosed with cancer. And it's wonderful that you want to help somebody who's sick. I just think you might want to think about it."

Ping. Back to Bailey.

"Mom," shouted Bailey. "There's nothing to think

about! If I cut it now I'll just have to throw it away! *Care Through Hair* doesn't want hair with lice!"

At the word *lice*, everything stopped. Olivia stopped pinging and ponging and held her orange head perfectly still. Bailey and her mom stopped yelling. The only sound in the room was a nervous chirp from Apollo.

"Maybe I should go," said Olivia finally. She put the dog down on the floor and stood up. "I gotta walk Shackleton."

"Wait," said Bailey. "I'll come with!"

"No, you won't," said Bailey's mom. "Listen, I think the idea of—lice— has us both a little freaked out. And I'm getting a little ahead of myself. Of course we can try getting rid of them first. That's why I came home early, isn't it? I got some special shampoo at the store. But I think we better get started, don't you, honeybee?"

Bailey did not think it was better to get started with the getting-rid-of-lice shampoo than to go with Olivia. But her mom was pinning her own hair up out of the way with a big silver clip, and Olivia was already at the door.

"Wait," said Bailey.

If she couldn't go with Olivia now, at least she could make a plan for later. It wasn't even really making the plan, since they did this every year around April eighteenth. It was more like checking on the plan.

"You're sleeping over Saturday, right? For my birthday?"

Olivia didn't answer right away, and in the silence that followed, Bailey started having the sand castle feeling again. A wave was coming. Not a regular wave. More like a tidal wave. She didn't need to hear Olivia's words to know what the answer was.

CHAPTER 5

· · · · · · · · · · · ·

This Was War

The answer had been no. Actually, it wasn't so much of a clear "no" as a shaky "I don't know." But a little later Olivia's mom had called to make it clear. Bailey was in the middle of the special shampoo, the part where the shampoo had to stay in for ten minutes, when the phone rang.

Bailey's mom picked up. She said yes. She said no. She said she totally understood. Then she switched off the phone.

"What?" asked Bailey. "What'd she say?"

"She said that she doesn't think a sleepover is a

good idea. And I said I agreed. She doesn't want to mess around with lice, and neither do I, honeybee."

The shampoo on Bailey's scalp stung. And it stank.

"So now what?" she asked.

Her mom shrugged. "Now I guess you have a daytime party. Olivia's mom said she wants to celebrate with you—of course she does—and that she can come over briefly if you have a party during the day."

"A daytime party, like you wanted me to have all along?" demanded Bailey.

"All I thought was that this year it might be nice to ask some *new* friends, instead of putting all your eggs in one basket, with Olivia."

"I'm not a chicken, Mom!"

"I know that, honeybee. But you haven't asked anybody out to the island all year. Maybe this birthday is a good time to . . . branch out a little."

"I'm not a tree, Mom!"

Bailey's mom sighed. "I know you're not a tree. And I know you're not a chicken. And nothing I thought or said about your birthday really matters anymore. Now you have lice, and a sleepover is out of the question."

Bailey could tell that this was one of those times when the moms had made an instant pact not to budge. The timer on the stove beeped. The ten stinging, stinky minutes were up. Her mom turned the kitchen tap back on and pointed to the stream of water.

"End of conversation," she said. "Now rinse, please."

Bailey stuck her head under the running water, which made it pretty much impossible to talk, anyway. After that came the electric hair dryer on full blast while her mom dried her hair. And after that came the actual dead lice. End of conversation.

Her mom had run the special metal comb with extra-long teeth through Bailey's hair. When Bailey snuck a peek at the comb, her stomach did a quick flip-flop. Gross! The dead louse had six legs that ended in pincers, like miniature lobster claws. Sextuple gross!

By the time the combing was finished, Bailey's mom

had pulled out four more dead lice, which she flushed down the toilet. She explained that this wasn't the end, though. According to the instructions they would have to use the special shampoo again in a week. Bailey would be glad when the week was over.

Then—because she didn't have much choice anymore—she had printed out birthday party invitations. Her mom said that if she was asking anybody from school, she was asking everybody. She couldn't ask some kids in her class and not others. Bailey could understand that it hurt kids' feelings to be left out. She got that. So she printed out enough invitations for everybody, and one more for Olivia.

She was sticking the invites in cubbies the next morning, when a kid she didn't recognize came into the class. Except he was wearing a shirt with the monarch butterfly life cycle on it.

"*Tucker?*" she asked, because he looked completely different.

He'd been buzzed.

Just then Mr. McGovern called everybody to the carpet for morning meeting.

"Remember, this is our time to share something, if we want, and to say good morning to each other." He picked a popsicle stick from a cup and read the name printed on it. "Tucker. Good morning, Tucker, How are you?"

"I got buzzed," announced Tucker, as if it wasn't obvious. "I didn't have lice, but my little sisters did. My mom says this is preventive."

Tucker wasn't the only kid with a new look. A couple more boys had been buzzed. A couple more girls wore bandannas, like Arianna. Emma and Rosa smelled like spaghetti. They had lice, too, but their mom didn't believe in using the shampoo you got from the store. She said it was like poison. Instead, she had slathered their heads in olive oil, so their hair looked sopping wet.

Mr. McGovern took a big positive-thinking breath. "I'm glad Tucker brought this up, so we can talk about what's happening in our class."

He began talking about how lice were parasites. They would die without their host. Their host: people. Specifically, people's heads. More specifically, the warm blood in people's heads.

Max shouted, "I *want* to *suck* your *blood*!" in a make-believe vampire voice.

"We're raising our hands before we talk," reminded Mr. McGovern, and then he went on with his life cycle of a louse lecture.

A louse crawls onto somebody's head. For the next few days it wanders around, sucking blood and laying eggs, which are called nits. The louse doesn't just put the eggs on the host's head like a chicken putting an egg in a nest, though. (David, Eli, and Joey made clucking noises until Mr. McGovern stared them down and continued.) The louse glues its eggs onto the host's hair so they won't fall off. Not just one or two eggs. Dozens. Maybe a hundred. After about a week, each nit hatches into a young louse, called a nymph. That nymph grows up into a louse, and the cycle begins again.

Mr. McGovern jumped up and grabbed a marker. "Let's wake up our brains with some math!"

Bailey did not want to wake up her brain with louse math. Because this was gross! She felt mad at Mr. M. How could he be so cheerful and positive about *lice*?

On the whiteboard, Mr. McGovern scribbled *1 louse = 100 nits.*

"Now, if each of those one hundred nits grows up and lays one hundred more nits, what do we have?"

Know-it-all Lexy's hand shot up in the air. "Ten thousand!"

Mr. McGovern beamed, as if the chance to combine science and math made it worth having bugs crawling all over Bailey's head. He was adding more zeroes to the whiteboard, showing how many lice that original louse could produce, and kids were shouting out numbers.

A million!

That was Emma.

A hundred million!

And Rosa.

A gazillion licillion!

And that was Tucker, who seemed as cheerful as Mr. McGovern. He didn't even seem mad about getting buzzed, which Bailey thought was crazy.

She had thought her mom was going a little crazy, yesterday, talking about cutting her hair. Now it turned out that some kids got haircuts even when they didn't have lice themselves. Just because of their sisters!

Bailey didn't have any brothers or sisters. Every once in a while her mom said, "Maybe I ought to have another baby so you don't end up spoiled rotten," but she never seemed to get around to it. Bailey figured that was because the way her mom had babies wasn't that easy.

Bailey's mom had wanted a baby so badly, she'd explained, but she wasn't married or anything close to married. So a doctor helped her have a baby. Which meant that Bailey didn't actually have a dad the same way most other kids did, and she never did get any brothers or sisters. Which suited Bailey just fine. It looked like brothers and sisters could make a lot of trouble. And instead of a dad, there was Aunt Jess.

Aunt Jess had helped convince Bailey's mom that it was okay to have a baby on her own. And she had been there when Bailey was born.

On the outside, Aunt Jess looked just like her sister, Bailey's mom. She wore big blouses and blue jeans and her hair was dark brown with silver streaks. But on the inside, she was totally different. She never tried to make things—like Bailey's life—"shipshape." Her "great ideas" never turned out badly for Bailey. They turned out great. Like her idea for how to spend Bailey's last birthday.

Bailey and Olivia had taken the morning boat to town, where Aunt Jess met them. First stop was the salon where Jess worked. It was a Sunday and the shop was closed, so they had the place to themselves. Aunt Jess turned up the music, washed and dried Bailey's hair (no cut, since she was already growing it out), and put in purple highlights. Olivia got her hair braided in about a hundred little braids, with a tiny bead at the end of each one. Next stop: waffles. With strawberries. *And* whipped cream. Third stop: the pet store. They got a cage and a water bottle and a bag of food, and then Bailey had picked lemon-and-lime Apollo from the flock of budgies. Finally, she and Olivia—and Apollo—had ridden the ferry back home in time for the sleepover.

Now that was Bailey's idea of a good idea.

"Good morning, Bailey. Is there anything you want to share?"

Bailey looked around. She'd been spacing out. Lice math seemed to be over. Mr. McGovern was back in the circle, doing good mornings. Everybody was looking at her, waiting for her to share.

"Bailey?" asked Mr. McGovern. "We're sharing now."

"Um—I put invites in everybody's cubby. For my birthday. On Saturday."

Quickly Mr. McGovern raised his hand high in the air—his silent call for silence—but it was too late. Everybody began chattering, because a party was better than just cupcakes in class. A party meant cake, too.

Bailey wasn't chattering. She was thinking.

She knew that people thought she was stubborn. And that really bugged her. That was just the way she was. And besides, who cared?

But as much as she didn't like it when people complained that she was stubborn, she knew it was true. Sometimes she could even feel something growing in her that she was going to be stubborn about. Like now.

Tucker might not care about his hair, but Bailey cared about hers. She was growing it for Aunt Jess. Well, not *for* Aunt Jess, exactly—it wasn't like Bailey's hair would make the wig that Aunt Jess might wear— but *because* of her. She might have had to change her birthday plans because of the lice, but there was no way she was going to change her plan to donate her hair to

Care Through Hair. No way was she going to let the lice win.

Now she got how Mr. Adams felt about the caterpillars making cobwebby tents in the trees.

This was war.

CHAPTER 6

The Lousiest Birthday

Saturday was warm—sweatshirt weather—and kids with scooters were suddenly everywhere, like the daffodils. It was so warm that the Snack Shack's windows were wide open, and Bailey could smell banana bread baking. People milled around the wharf, chatting and sipping coffee in the sunshine. A big blue jay swooped overhead. It was spring.

April eighteenth, to be exact, and Bailey was waiting for the boat that would bring the kids from her class to the island. She could see the yellow dot that was the ferry, crossing the bay. She hoped Olivia got here before the boat did.

"Hey!" called a voice, and Olivia came running up. She paused to catch her breath.

"Hey," echoed Bailey. "What's up?"

"What's up is it's your birthday," said Olivia. She handed Bailey a wrapped present. "So happy birthday!"

Bailey took the present but didn't open it. That would come later. "Thanks," she said.

"Sorry about the sleepover," said Olivia. "But my mom was like—*no way*. She said if I got—you know— she'd have an easy solution." Grinning, she pointed to her golden orange hair, which was pulled back into a tiny bun. "Off. All of it."

"You said you hated your hair," Bailey pointed out.

Olivia shrugged. "Yeah!" she agreed. "But bad hair is better than no hair!"

Bailey couldn't argue with that. And it wasn't Olivia's fault that the moms had vetoed this year's sleepover. She just wished that when Olivia said *Sorry*, she sounded like she meant it, instead of sounding like it wasn't a big deal. Which it was, to Bailey.

"So who's coming?" asked Olivia.

"I'm not totally sure," said Bailey.

The school had the same rule as her mom: You could only use the class cubbies to invite people to your birthday if you included everybody. So plenty of kids invited the whole class to their party. It never meant that the whole class went, though. Bailey knew that because of all the times she'd been asked but hadn't gone. Like the parties for David or Eli or Joey. Those were just following-the-rule invitations. They didn't really want her to come and she didn't really want to go. No big deal, for real.

But now it was her party. Deal.

At recess she hung out with Rashad, or sometimes Emma and Rosa. If they got to pick partners for learning buddies she tried to team up with Max, who was smart and not too bossy. Or sometimes Emma or Rosa. She bet those kids would come.

The Lousiest Birthday

Here came the ferry now—big and yellow with its name printed in black letters on the side—the *State of Maine*. As soon as it docked, people started shuffling off with their groceries and dogs and bicycles. Bailey scanned the crowd for kids she knew.

Above the heads of the crowd, a blue balloon was bobbing up and down. It was getting closer. And the hand holding onto the string was . . .

Tucker Pierce.

"Yo!" he said as he spotted her and handed her the balloon. "This is for you. I know it's stupid, but my mom made me bring it. So happy birthday!"

"Happy birthday," echoed a voice, not sounding happy at all.

It was Lexy Nguyen with her arm in a sling and her head in a bandanna.

"What happened to you?" asked Bailey.

"She broke her wrist yesterday. Plus she has lice," offered Tucker, whose shirt today was printed with different species of ants.

"So I couldn't go to gymnastics today," pouted Lexy. "So I came here instead."

"Wow. That's—too bad," said Bailey.

"Hey," said a small voice.

It was Arianna Fogelman, standing quietly to the side. As usual, she had on her purple glasses and her leopard-print bandanna.

"Happy birthday!" she managed.

"Thanks," said Bailey, and looked around for the others.

There were no others. This was it. Know-it-all Lexy Nguyen. Quiet Arianna Fogelman, louse expert. And bug-crazy Tucker Pierce, the most annoying boy in fifth grade. Out of twenty kids in her class, only three had shown up. Half of Bailey was surprised. But the other half was saying, Told you so! Everybody from school was a during-school friend. She hadn't really tried to be better friends with anybody. After-school friends. Weekend friends. She had kept after school and weekends for Olivia.

Who was standing there, not saying anything. Then Bailey had a lightbulb moment: introductions! Olivia didn't know anybody.

"Hey, you guys, this is my friend Olivia. This is Lexy and Arianna and Tucker."

Lexy and Arianna and Tucker all said hi. Olivia gave a tiny hi wave back. For a minute nobody seemed to know what to say, until Tucker broke the silence.

"So what do we do now?" he asked. "What's the plan?"

Good idea—the plan. The plan was to go back to the house. Have lunch and cake. Walk around the island, maybe stopping to explore the old fort. Then put kids on the three o'clock boat back to the mainland.

Step one of the plan: Bailey took them home, where her mom poured glasses of lemonade and served up pizza and then said, "Tell me about the scarves, girls. Is that the new style? Or is it some kind of club?"

Tucker helped himself to a second piece of pizza. "Club Lice!"

Lexy stuck her tongue out at Tucker. "It's 'cause I have lice," she said to Bailey's mom. "And my mom doesn't want my little sisters to get them."

"I *don't* have lice," boasted Arianna. "And this way I won't get them."

"What a great idea!" said Bailey's mother. "Bailey, maybe you should be wearing one."

"No, Mom," said Bailey quickly, "not a great idea," but it was too late. Her mom had already left the room in search of a scarf.

Lexy turned to Bailey. "I wouldn't have to wear this stupid thing if it wasn't for you! You probably gave them to me!"

"Says who?" asked Bailey. "Maybe you gave them to me!"

"You had them first!" hissed Lexy.

Bailey defended herself. "It's not my fault! The nurse said they were going around the whole school!"

Lexy opened her mouth to fight back, but then

closed it as Bailey's mom returned with two bandannas and a painter's hat.

"You have a choice," she said. "Red, white, or blue."

Bailey's mom was a big believer in choices.

"Neither," said Bailey.

"That's not one of the choices," said her mom. "Pick a color, honeybee, and then it's time for cake."

Did her mom think she was a baby, ready to be bribed by cake? Bailey was insulted. She was also not into having a big fight with her mom in front of everybody.

"Red," she said. She folded the bandanna square into a triangle, and tied it on.

"What about you, Olivia?" asked Bailey's mom. "An ounce of prevention is worth a pound of cure."

"White, please," said Olivia, and tucked her orange bun up underneath the painter's cap.

Tucker grabbed a third piece of pizza. "I feel left out! Can I be in the club?"

Bailey's mom gave Tucker a big smile, and the blue bandanna.

"How do I look?" he asked, when he'd tied it on over his buzz cut.

"Ridiculous," declared Lexy. "Just like the rest of us."

"You look kind of like a pirate," said Arianna.

Olivia giggled. "A pizza-eating pirate?"

"Aargh!" shouted Tucker. "Shiver me timbers! Walk the plank! Avast there, ye landlubbers, 'tis time for cake!"

Bailey's mom had lit the candles and was carrying over the cake. Everybody sang "Happy Birthday," and Apollo chirped along.

"Happy birthday, honeybee," said Bailey's mom as she set the cake down in front of Bailey. "Wait—let me get a picture of you and the cake and everybody in their headgear." She grabbed her camera. "This has got to be the funniest birthday ever."

"Don't you mean *lousiest*?" demanded Tucker. "Get it? A louse makes it lousy? Get it? Get it?"

"We get it, Tucker," said Lexy, sounding as annoyed as Bailey felt.

Olivia got it, too, but she sounded more amused than annoyed. "I never knew that's where *lousy* came from!"

Bailey's mom snapped the picture, and Bailey blew out the candles on her cake. Yellow with chocolate frosting. Her favorite. At least the cake wasn't lousy.

Bailey sat and ate her cake, listening to Olivia joke around with Tucker, Lexy, and Arianna. These were the kids Olivia would have known already, if she'd gone to Casco Elementary like they planned. Olivia could have made friends with them last fall. She could make friends with them next fall, in middle school. How come she had to make friends with them *now*, at Bailey's party?

And how come she hadn't switched schools, anyway? Olivia had never really given Bailey a good reason for not wanting to make the switch. Before, it seemed like she'd always wanted to do whatever Bailey wanted to do. Hanging out together every day after school. Roaming the beach, searching tide pools for starfish and fiddler crabs. Or staying home and making chocolate chip pancakes.

Bailey took another lick of chocolate frosting. She knew it was babyish, not wanting to share Olivia, but that's how she felt. She also felt like she'd eaten her cake too fast. Her stomach hurt. She put down her plate and went and sat by Apollo's cage.

Apollo started chirping again.

A soft voice said, "He's so pretty."

It was Arianna. She came and sat down beside Bailey. "What's his name?"

"Apollo," came Olivia's voice, before Bailey could answer.

Now Bailey really felt annoyed. It was bad enough Olivia was glomming onto her friends, but did she have to act all possessive about Apollo, too?

"Apollo," said Bailey, as if it hadn't already been

said. She held a spray of millet seed through the cage bars. "Step up!" she coaxed.

"Step up?" asked Arianna.

"That's how you call a bird," said Bailey. "You say, 'Step up!'"

She explained how there were about five parts to hand-taming a bird. First you got the bird to eat the food in your hand, with the cage bars in between. That was the step she was on right now.

After the bird got used to that, you put your hand *inside* the cage. Then, day by day, you made the millet spray shorter and shorter. Gradually, the bird got closer and closer until he was eating right from your hand. The whole time, you kept asking the bird to "step up." And by the end, the bird would land on your finger. Hopefully.

As she finished explaining, Apollo started to nibble seeds from the millet spray, just like he was supposed to. Bailey felt hope light up inside her with a flicker, like a birthday candle. Maybe she really could teach Apollo to sit on her hand. And maybe—what she really wanted—she could teach him in time to show Aunt Jess next time she came to the island.

"Step up," said Bailey, and Apollo stopped nibbling, tilted his yellow head at her, and gave a little answering chirp.

Olivia bent her head in its white painter's cap up close to the cage and crooned, "Hey, pretty boy."

Then Arianna leaned in with her leopard bandanna and purple glasses. "Pretty boy," she cooed softly. "Pretty boy."

Apollo chirped again, more loudly this time.

"I think you're too close," said Bailey. "You're scaring him. And I need some room for the next step."

Arianna and Olivia moved back a respectful distance.

This was crazy. She and Apollo weren't ready. There were about five steps before you could put your hand in with no food and have the bird land on it, and she and Apollo were still on the first one.

A voice inside was shouting *don't do it!* but her hand was moving anyway, like it didn't care what the voice said.

Bailey opened the cage door just wide enough to slip her hand inside. She whistled softly. "Step up! Come on, Apollo. Step up!"

The next few things happened so quickly that Bailey was never sure exactly what happened when. It was all scrambled together in one horrible, chaotic moment.

The door to the cage opened wider and Apollo flew out and fluttered wildly around the kitchen. Somebody's feet pounded up the porch steps, and the kitchen door swung open as Zach Sawyer shouted, "Happy Birthday, Bai-ee!" And Apollo's lemon yellow head and lime green wings disappeared out the open door and into the bright blue sky.

CHAPTER 7

· · · · · · · · · · · · · ·

Invasion of the Creepy Crawlies

I
t felt like when a wave caught you by surprise and
you swallowed water and you couldn't breathe
right. Apollo!

Finally, with a gasp, Bailey took a tiny breath and
then held it, trying to hold back her tears.

It wasn't working. Everything was starting to look
all swimmy, like she'd opened her eyes underwater.
But Bailey couldn't cry now. Not in front of everyone.
Besides, Zach was crying enough for both of them. Not
just crying. Sobbing. He thought it was all his fault.

She crouched down so she was face-to-face with

Zach. "It's not your fault, Zach," she said. "Buddy, you hear me? It's not your fault."

But Zach was beyond hearing. He'd gone into a bad crying place. Bailey had seen this before. He would cry until he passed out. Apologizing, his mom scooped him up, promised to call if she saw Apollo anywhere, and left.

Bailey grabbed the butterfly net and hurried out the door, with Tucker, Lexy, Arianna, and Olivia right behind.

Think: what would a bird that had always lived in a cage do? Would he find a branch and not move? Would he fly from tree to tree? Slowly, she walked around the yard. She walked with her head tilted up, looking into the trees. The trees weren't totally bare, like in winter, but they weren't covered in green leaves, either, like in summer. They were spring trees, their leaves still wrapped up tight, the color of caramel. If a yellow and green budgie was perched on one of those branches, you could probably see it.

Except they didn't see any sign of a yellow and green budgie.

They searched the nearby road. Still no sign of Apollo.

They went farther, up and down the lanes and roads that crisscrossed the middle of the island. They saw one cardinal, two blue jays, a few robins and red-winged blackbirds. But no budgie. They walked the island's perimeter on Big Loop and saw countless seagulls. But no budgie. They were walking the smaller circle of Little Loop, going past the Historical Society when Mr. Adams called out.

"If it isn't Bailey and Olivia! Good afternoon, good afternoon."

Bailey was tired. She stopped to talk. "Hey, Mr. Adams," she said. "How's the war with the tent caterpillars going?"

Mr. Adams twisted the ends of his curlicue mustache. "I haven't achieved complete eradication of those pests," he said. "But the battle isn't over!"

Suddenly Mr. Adams stopped crimping his mustache and did a double take, looking slowly from kid to kid.

"May I inquire as to the nature of your . . ." he trailed off, pointing at their heads.

"Lice!" said Tucker cheerfully. "Bailey and Lexy have lice."

Lexy scolded Tucker that he didn't have to tell the world, while Arianna and Olivia clarified that they *didn't* have lice. Their head coverings were preventive. The whole time Mr. Adams was nodding his head sympathetically.

"It was a tremendous problem in the Revolutionary War armies," he said. "I wrote an entire paper on it for the *Historical Journal*. Our soldiers not only had to fight the British, they had to combat lice and fleas and all manner of pestilence."

Tucker said, "Cool!"

Lexy said doubtfully, "I never heard that before."

And Bailey, trying to be polite, said, "Really?"

"Yes, yes, indeed," said Mr. Adams. "Poor George Washington. Very difficult to keep up troop morale under an onslaught of *Pediculus humanus capitis*."

"That's Latin for lice!" cried Lexy.

"Of course, General Washington took strength in knowing he was working for a noble cause," observed Mr. Adams.

Tucker struck what Bailey assumed was his attempt at a noble pose and recited everything he knew about the American Revolution, in no particular order. "No taxation without representation! Give me liberty or give me death! One if by land and two if by sea!"

"A budding historian!" beamed Mr. Adams, studying Tucker. "Marvelous!"

"Well, we gotta go, Mr. Adams," said Bailey. "Come on, you guys."

They had only gone about three steps when Mr. Adams remembered one more thing. "Wait!" he called. "Wait just a moment, please. May I also inquire, are you newcomers all in Bailey's class?"

Tucker and Lexy and Arianna all said yes.

"Fifth graders, then? Studying the American Revolution?"

Again they said yes, and Mr. Adams got a wild look in his eye.

"Are you thinking what I'm thinking?" he asked Bailey.

All Bailey was thinking about was that she needed to get back to searching for Apollo.

"We really gotta go, Mr. Adams. I'm looking for my bird, Apollo. He escaped."

Mr. Adams gasped in true sympathy and looked like he might be about to launch into a lecture on birds and the American Revolution.

"My sympathies!" he cried, only briefly sidetracked. "But I am thinking," he said, "that this is a unique opportunity to do something really magnificent! How many students are in your class?"

"Twenty," volunteered Tucker. "How come?"

Mr. Adams started telling Tucker, Lexy, and

Arianna all about the Historical Society. How every year the society reenacted an event from the American Revolution. How he—as the president—got to pick the event. How he wanted to do something really spectacular because it was the society's fiftieth anniversary and they were expecting an extra-large turnout of old friends and members of other historical societies from all over New England. And how usually they depended on the island fifth graders . . .

He turned to Olivia. "What do you think, Miss Olivia? Could we use a little more help this year, from these young historians across the sea?"

"Sure," said Olivia with a shrug. "Sounds fun."

Bailey listened in a daze. Mr. Adams was thinking about asking her whole class to take part in Reenactment Day? But Reenactment Day was for fifth graders in Fox Island Elementary. And her, because she lived here. And maybe inviting Tucker, Lexy, and Arianna wasn't such a bad idea. They had come to her party. They had trekked all over the island, helping her look for Apollo. But why should the rest of the kids in her class, the ones who didn't even come to her party, get to come for Reenactment Day? Bailey knew she was being babyish again, but that's how she felt. How she felt was: no way! The island would be crawling with kids who she *didn't* want. Uninvited guests.

Looks like you have some uninvited guests! remembered Bailey, and right away wished she hadn't. Just thinking about lice made her head itch. She reached up underneath her bandanna to scratch. Why was she so itchy again? What if the shampoo hadn't worked? Or what if somebody else's lice had crawled onto her since the shampoo?

When you itched like crazy, it made you *feel* crazy. It made you feel like you were watching a scary movie. *The Invasion of the Creepy Crawlies.* But you couldn't turn it off and stop watching, because you were *inside* the movie. Creepy crawlies are invading the island! Creepy crawlies are on your head! There is no escape!

Bailey couldn't take it anymore. She interrupted Mr. Adams.

"The boat," she warned.

That was all she needed to say. Everybody got that you couldn't miss your boat. Mr. Adams promised to be in touch after he had considered more fully this unique opportunity, and then—*finally*—waved them on. Then Olivia promised to call if she saw any sign of Apollo, but said she was supposed to be home already. She better go. So at the next crossroads, she peeled off in one direction and Bailey went in another, walking Tucker, Lexy, and Arianna to the boat. They all waved to her as the *State of Maine* pulled away from the island and started across the bay.

Bailey waved back, then turned for home. She didn't really want to get there, though—see Apollo's empty cage—and she walked slowly, taking tiny steps. Thinking about the day. How easy it was to have the worst birthday of your life.

Step one: Have your mom nix your birthday plan,

so you're forced to ask a bunch of kids you don't really want. Then have only three of those kids show up.

Step two: Do something really stupid, so your bird escapes. Your bird that your aunt gave you.

Step three: Have crazy old Mr. Adams have the brilliant idea of inviting your entire class out to the island. Including all the kids who had blown off your birthday.

The worst, stupidest, craziest, itchiest, lousiest birthday of your life.

CHAPTER 8

Everybody's Different!

unday morning Bailey got up early, gobbled down some leftover pizza for breakfast, and grabbed her hoodie.

"Hold your horses," said her mother. "Where do you think you're going?"

"To look for Apollo."

"We have church, remember?"

"Mom!" said Bailey. "I can't go today! I have to find Apollo!"

"Honeybee," said her mom, "I know how worried you are, and I hope more than anything that you can find him. But you can start looking after church. An hour or two won't make much difference."

"Mom! Why can't I miss just this once?"

"You know why," said her mom. "You made a commitment to the choir director."

Bailey couldn't believe this. If a kid made up their mind about something, the parent called the kid stubborn. But if a grown-up made up their mind about something they wanted their kid to do, they didn't call it being stubborn. They called it a *commitment*.

Half an hour later Bailey was fulfilling her commitment to the choir director. She marched in with the choir, two by two, like the girls in *Madeline*. She wore a long blue robe on top of her clothes and the red bandanna on top of her head. Her neck felt itchy and she wished she could scratch, but that was pretty much impossible when you were carrying a hymnal and singing *Joyful, joyful, we adore thee* with fifty people watching you.

She marched along beside Olivia. They always

paired up because they were the same height and both sang soprano.

"Teach us how to love each other, lift us to the joy divine," they finished, and then the minister welcomed everybody, and then everybody sat down.

Bailey sat next to Olivia. She was definitely not loving Olivia right now, like the song said they should. She was not even liking her.

Nothing had gone the way Bailey had planned this year. She had planned on going to Casco Elementary with Olivia. Hadn't happened. She'd planned on staying best friends with Olivia anyway. Also didn't happen. It had been not happening all year, Bailey guessed, but she hadn't known it for sure until now. Now it was obvious. Because her old best friend would have slept over on her birthday. And even if the moms blocked the sleepover, her old best friend at least would have minded.

Bailey couldn't believe she had risked losing Apollo—and lost him—trying to . . . what? Impress

Everybody's Different!

Olivia? So she'd still want to be best friends? How stupid was that?

Bailey was mulling over how stupid she was, when Olivia pulled out the pen they kept hidden beneath their pew cushion, wrote something on her leaflet, and edged it toward Bailey.

Bailey read the note: *Sorry about Apollo.* And she couldn't help it. She felt hope lighting up inside her like one of those trick birthday candles. No matter how much you blew on them, they stayed lit. Because no matter what, there was still a part of her that wanted everything to be the way it used to be. The way things used to be was just . . . doing things together. Beachcombing at Driftwood Beach, searching for shells with holes so they could make necklaces. Weaving rainbow-colored pot holders for the church fair. Hanging out at the Snack Shack. Sleeping over.

Hopefully, she scribbled a reply. *Help me look for Apollo after church?*

Olivia was reaching for the pen when the choir

director's head appeared over the top of the organ. He shot them his special look—smiling mouth and glaring eyes. No more notes.

But Bailey knew another way. Last year, back when she was in fourth grade with Olivia, they had done a special unit called *Everybody's Different!* They had talked about different ways of communicating, like sign language. Bailey and Olivia used to practice together all the time. They got so good, the teacher even shot a video of them signing and put it on the school website. Bailey still remembered some of the signs. She put her hand flat on her heart, like if she was going to say the Pledge of Allegiance, but then she made little circles. That meant *Please*.

Olivia answered with a sign, too: circling her bunched-up fist on her chest. It was the sign for *Sorry*. Meaning, *No*.

"Sorry I can't help look for Apollo," explained Olivia after the service as they were hanging up their robes in the choir room. "Grandparents—command performance. You know how it is."

"Sure," said Bailey.

Even though she wasn't sure anymore, about Olivia. It seemed like all Olivia said was Sorry, I can't. But she didn't sound sorry. Maybe she was just using her grandparents as an excuse. Bailey didn't really know about grandparents, though. Her mom's parents lived in Florida and she hardly ever saw them. And there were no other grandparents because there wasn't another parent.

It was only weird when you thought about it. Like if you thought about the expression, *sides* of the family. A side always came in pairs. There was the right side and the left side. The mom's side and the dad's side. If you only had one side and not the other, was it still a side?

"Hello?" said Olivia. "Earth to Bailey? See you later, okay?"

Bailey stuck her sheet music and hymnal in her cubby. "Later," she agreed, as if that was okay with her. As if there actually was a plan to get together later.

Outside, the sun was shining in a sky the same bright blue as her choir robe. Bailey spent the rest of the day covering the same roads she'd covered yesterday—Big Loop and Little Loop and the roads through the middle of the island. She got an ache in her neck from walking with her head tilted up toward the treetops. It seemed like there were even more yellow daffodils blooming today than yesterday, and more birds singing. Walking in the sun, Bailey grew warm, and she took off her hoodie and wrapped it around her waist.

Warm was good, right? Apollo needed the weather to stay warm. But was it warm enough for a tropical bird? And what about food? Would he find the seeds that people put out for the wild birds? Would he find the birdbaths full of fresh water?

At least he couldn't go far. At least, she didn't *think*

he could go very far. Bailey didn't know exactly how far a budgie could fly. He wouldn't set out over the water, would he? Budgerigars didn't migrate across oceans; they stayed where they lived. He had to be somewhere on the island. Somewhere she could find him. And she had to find him soon. Walking, Bailey ticked off all the possible dangers. No food. No water. Too cold. She didn't even want to think about predators. Hawks and cats.

The last place Bailey went was the wharf, where she put a "lost bird" sign on the community bulletin board. By then it was getting late, and she gave up for the day and went home, where her mother announced grimly that it was time to wash her hair with the special shampoo again.

This would be the second treatment. Apparently the shampoo could kill crawling-around lice, but not nits. So you shampooed once, and then again a week later, to zap any lice that had hatched since the first treatment. Then—just to be on the safe side—you had to keep searching for any last lice that might still be hiding, safe inside their eggs.

Leaning over the kitchen sink, Bailey felt the warm water cascade over her head, and her mom's fingers scratching and scrubbing. Then her mom dried her hair with the electric dryer, and began the search for nits. While her mom searched, tugging and pulling through Bailey's hair, Bailey sat.

And sat.

And sat.

Her mom kept pausing to study the instructions that came with the shampoo—there was a picture of a nit glued to a hair shaft—and muttering about looking for a needle in a haystack.

Finally, after what felt like an hour, her mom said, "I'm done. I guess."

"You guess?" asked Bailey, alarmed.

What was that supposed to mean? She was counting

on her mom cleaning her head the same way she made people's houses spick-and-span.

"What do you mean, you guess?"

"I mean that I hope the shampoo did its job. And if there were any leftover nits, I hope I got them. It's just hard to know for sure. They're so tiny. It's so . . ." Her mom trailed off, searching for the right word. "Nitpicky!"

She sounded like she wanted to laugh and cry at the same time.

Bailey did not want to laugh. Because having lice was *not* funny. She didn't want to cry, either. She just wanted this to be over! No more itching. No more bandanna. No more lice.

CHAPTER 9

Lemonade

The next morning began week two of the Casco Elementary louse infestation, which the nurse said was the worst she had ever seen. And until the infestation was definitely over, Bailey's mom had decided that Bailey should keep wearing a bandanna. If Bailey still had lice, it would stop her from spreading them to other kids. And it would stop other kids from giving lice to her. Hopefully.

Apparently other kids' parents felt the same way. Every day more kids came to school with some kind of louse-prevention hairdo. A buzz cut, bandanna, or braids. By the end of the week the only kids who didn't have a new look were a couple of boys who already had supershort hair, and Rashad and a couple other girls who already wore a headscarf every day for their religion.

Mr. McGovern—who was taking so many positive-thinking breaths Bailey was afraid he might hyperventilate—said this was an opportunity to *stretch* their thinking. A real lemons-into-lemonade situation, he said. Sure, lemons were sour, but you could make lemonade from them! Bailey did not think that an in-depth study of lice qualified as "lemonade," but she didn't have much choice. Language Arts was now writing about lice. Math was multiplying big numbers of theoretical lice populations. Science was looking at the amazing life cycle of lice and other parasites.

Mr. M. was so busy making lemonade out of the louse infestation that he seemed to have forgotten all about their unit on American history. Bailey hoped

Mr. Adams had forgotten all about his latest American history idea, too. Didn't old people forget things sometimes? Or maybe he was so busy with his war on the tent caterpillars that he didn't have time to explore any unique opportunities, like infesting Fox Island with the Casco fifth graders.

Bailey was busy, too. All week at school she was busy studying lice. Every day after school she hit the island roads, looking for Apollo.

On Friday afternoon a steady drizzle was falling from a dull gray sky into a dull gray ocean. Everyone hurried off the ferry, not stopping to chat. A few gulls huddled on the shoreline, too bedraggled to bother with their usual squawking. Bailey decided on a short detour before she started searching.

A little bell jingled when she pushed open the door of the Snack Shack. Inside it was warm and steamy from treats baking and people talking. There was Mr. Walker, whose name fit him perfectly: He was eighty-eight and still circled the island every single day. There was Bruce Levinsky, who painted houses, in his paint-splattered clothes, and Mrs. Webster, the librarian, who always stopped in on double-fudge brownie Fridays. And there were Aidan, Hayden, and Sam, the entire Fox Island fifth-grade class, minus Olivia. They were sitting in the corner window.

Bailey got a double-fudge brownie at the counter, slung her backpack under the table, and slid in next to Sam. "Hey," she said, "where's Olivia?"

Sam shrugged. "She said she had to get right home, or something."

"Hey," said Aidan, "is it true you're doing Reenactment Day with us?"

"Is it true the other kids from your class might do it, too?" asked Hayden.

"Is it true you lost your bird?" asked Sam.

Bailey gulped down a big bite of brownie. This was one part of the island school she'd wanted to get away from. The part where everybody was into everybody's business.

"Is that what Olivia told you?" she asked.

"She only told us about your bird," said Sam.

"We found out about the reenactment all on our own," put in Aidan. "Mr. Adams came to talk to Ms. Doyle today, and we sort of heard them."

Hayden boasted, "We were sort of listening."

"You mean eavesdropping!" said Sam, who was a little hyper about rules.

Hayden objected, "But they always tell us to use our listening ears!"

"Whatever," said Bailey, wondering what Ms. Doyle had thought about Mr. Adams's idea. Maybe she wouldn't like it. Or maybe Mr. McGovern wouldn't. Except Ms. Doyle liked everything Mr. Adams did. And Mr. M. liked *all* new ideas.

"That'd be cool if they did come," said Aidan.

"Wicked," agreed Hayden.

Bailey wasn't so sure it sounded wicked cool for the kids from her new school to join the kids from her old school. It sounded . . . mixed up. The way her party had been. A mixed-up, total disaster.

"You think?" she asked.

Aidan shrugged like it was obvious. "It'll be way better with more kids."

Hayden backed him up with a "Duh!" and Aidan backed up Hayden with "Double duh!"

"But Reenactment Day is an island thing," she said.

"So how is that fair?" demanded Sam. "*You're* not in the island school."

Bailey circled her fingers on the foggy window to make a little spy-hole, but all she could see was rain dripping down the outside of the glass. "But I live here," she said.

"Big whoop," said Hayden.

"Jumbo whoop," agreed Aidan.

They started making *whoop-whoop-whooping* noises until Mrs. Webster, the librarian, shushed them, while Sam pointed out, "That's, like, totally hypocritical."

Bailey took another bite of brownie so she wouldn't have to answer. Because Sam's point was a little too . . . pointy. It felt like the last time she'd gone to the doctor's and had to have a shot. A shot didn't just sting going in. It stayed sore after, too.

That whole last week of summer, after Olivia had changed her mind and decided to stay in the island school, she kept trying to talk Bailey into staying. And Bailey just kept trying to talk Olivia into going. But for once Olivia didn't want to do the exact same thing Bailey was doing. For once she was being just as stubborn as Bailey.

So on the first day of fifth grade Bailey had boarded the ferry by herself, thinking she could go away and everything here would stay the same. Which she now realized was, like, totally hypocritical. Sure, Olivia could have come with her. And Bailey was still sore that she hadn't. But Bailey *could* have stayed here, too. If she'd stayed here, maybe she and Olivia would still be best friends. And Reenactment Day would be the island fifth graders, just like always, instead of all mixed up. Messed up. Because of her.

"Hey," said Sam suddenly. "Total bummer about your bird!"

"Bummer," agreed Aidan.

"Totally," added Hayden.

"Thanks," said Bailey.

She slipped out from the window seat and grabbed her backpack, saying she had to go look for Apollo— which was true, even if it wasn't the whole truth. There was something else she needed to do, too.

The Snack Shack's bell jingled behind her as she stepped outside, where the drizzle had made up its mind to become a real rain shower. Bailey pulled up the hood of her sweatshirt, which didn't help much. Rain dribbled from the sky onto the trees and dropped from the trees onto the ground—and onto Bailey—as she walked the familiar roads. By the time she got to Olivia's she was soaked. She knocked, and waited. She could feel the straps of her backpack digging into her back, but she didn't take it off. She didn't know if she was staying.

Finally the door swung open and a voice came through the screen door. "Bai-ee!"

"Zach!" she said.

Zach? What was Zach doing *here* on a Friday— one of *her* days?

"Hey!" said Olivia as she came up behind the little boy. She looked all blurry through the screen. "We're going to stay *inside*, Zach. Because it's *raining*."

Bailey didn't know what to say. She could practically hear the words Olivia meant but didn't say out loud to the little boy: *because the person on the porch has lice and your mom'll kill me if you get them, too.* Luckily Zach filled the silence by chiming in with "Ay-ning, ay-ning!" He liked to say everything twice.

"It *is* raining!" agreed Bailey.

Olivia started talking nonstop, like soda bubbling over. "Mrs. Sawyer wanted me to try babysitting here," she explained, "so she gets a little more peace and quiet, and my mom's around for backup. Plus she asked if I could take your days, but it's just temporary! She said you could have your days back as soon as you were—ready. You mad?"

For a second Bailey was too surprised to say anything, and the only sound was the drip-dropping rain and Zach zipping his fingertips back and forth on the screen. Then she shook her head. It wasn't Olivia's fault that Mrs. Sawyer gave her Bailey's babysitting days. Besides, *she* was the one who should be saying sorry. It was time to do what she'd come here to do. Get it over with. She said the words so quickly that they were all jumbled together.

"Sorry-I-didn't-stay-this-year," she blurted.

Through the screen door, inside her halo of orange hair, Olivia's face brightened. "Me too. I mean, not *you*—" She started babbling again. "*Me*. Sorry I didn't go."

Bailey shook her head again. "No, I should've stayed."

Olivia shrugged. "Or I should've gone."

"What's it like this year?"

"Boring. What's Casco like?"

Trying to think how to describe her new school, Bailey grinned as she came up with the perfect answer. "Lousy."

Olivia laughed. "Promise I'll go to middle school with you."

Since there wasn't a middle school on the island, Olivia didn't have much choice, but Bailey got it. She had made a joke, and Olivia had made a joke, and it felt like they had made up. Bailey felt better now. But not *all better*. She was still standing out here on the porch, looking at Olivia through the crisscross lines of the screen door. Not being invited in. Her backpack felt heavy and her sneakers were sopping wet.

"So, any luck with . . . " Olivia paused.

Bailey knew how to fill in the blank: any luck with Apollo. Olivia was smart not to say the bird's name. She couldn't risk a Zach-attack meltdown.

Bailey shook her head. "Not yet."

"I'm really sorry," said Olivia.

"It's not *your* fault," said Bailey. "I was the one who—you know."

"I'm still sorry," insisted Olivia. "I hope you find— it. Then you can use . . ." She drifted off, searching for a Zach-approved way to say something. Her face lit up as she figured it out: Cupping her hands, she moved them toward Bailey, and then back again.

Bailey remembered that sign. It meant a *present*. What present? She made the sign herself, and then drew the question mark sign in the air.

Olivia signed *present* again and then looked stumped, like she couldn't remember the sign for something. Finally she used the alphabet signs to spell out the word: *P . . . A . . . R . . . T . . . Y.*

Party . . . present . . . Olivia's gift for her birthday! Bailey had never opened it! Somehow, between rushing out to search for Apollo that day and then dealing with lice all week, she had forgotten all about it. She couldn't say that to Olivia, though. So she nodded, as if she knew what Olivia meant, put her palm to her mouth and lowered her hand: *Thank you.*

"I better go look for—you know." She left out Apollo's name. "So . . . bye."

"Bye," echoed Olivia, as Bailey stepped off the porch, while Zach madly chirped, "Bye-bye! Bye-bye!"

When she got home she found the kitchen chairs piled with dirty laundry, and clean laundry stacked on the dining table. For the last few days Bailey's mom had been in lice eradication overdrive. She was washing every single piece of fabric in the house, and anything used daily, like towels and pillowcases, was getting washed daily.

"Mom!" called Bailey. "Mom, where's Olivia's present?"

Her mom came into the kitchen, holding a bulging trash bag. "Good question," she said. "The gifts never got opened, did they, what with all the . . . commotion.

Now where did they end up?" She set down the bag and started looking under piles of laundry.

"What's in here?" asked Bailey. She took a look in the bag. "My stuffed animals!"

Bailey's mom kept searching as she explained. All the literature on lice said it was a good idea to wash or otherwise delouse anything that could harbor a louse egg. Including stuffed animals. She wasn't going to get rid of them; she was just going to put them in the basement. For the time being. When the lice were gone, Bailey could have the animals back. If she still wanted them.

"I do!" protested Bailey. "How could you think I didn't want them?"

"Maybe because you haven't played with them in months!" snapped Bailey's mom. She kept lifting things up and setting them down, until finally she found the presents underneath a stack of newspapers. "What are they doing here?" she cried. "This house is a wreck."

Bailey reached for the box Olivia had shown her at the wharf, took off the wrapping paper, and looked inside.

It was a swing for Apollo.

"Oh, honey," said her mom sadly.

Bailey couldn't answer. She opened the door of the aviary and stepped inside. The food dishes were still full of seed and the bottle was full of water. Reaching up, she hung the swing from one of the tree branches. It swung back and forth a few times, and then stopped.

CHAPTER 10

The Mayonnaise Method

I just don't understand," grumbled Bailey's mom. "How can you still have nits?"

It was Sunday night. Two whole weeks since the first treatment with the special shampoo. One week since the follow-up treatment. According to the instructions, the lice should be gone. But the nitpicking was turning up nits.

"How should I know?" said Bailey.

"Well, all I know is, where there's smoke, there's fire."

"What's that supposed to mean?"

"I don't know whether the shampoo didn't work, or if a new *critter* crawled onto you since then, but *something* is laying eggs in your hair. Bailey—honeybee. I'm afraid a louse is hiding somewhere in this long mane of yours."

Bailey saw where that was going. Quickly she said, "I'm not cutting my hair. You can't make me."

"If it comes to that," said her mom, "I can. But I'd rather have you make the decision. You're old enough to figure this out for yourself."

That's what grown-ups said, when all they really meant was that you should decide to do what *they* wanted. They never suggested you were old enough to figure things out if you were going to do what *you* wanted. Which Bailey was. She was going to get rid of the lice and *then* cut her hair, so she could donate it. There was nothing to figure out.

But Bailey knew if she was going to get out of this argument, she better come up with something good.

"Mom," she said. "I made a commitment."

The Mayonnaise Method

That seemed to do the trick. Bailey's mom was a big believer in commitments, and she hadn't been too happy when the choir director had called to suggest that Bailey "take a little break" until her "situation was all cleared up." Bailey knew what that meant. Stay home until the lice are gone. So much for honoring commitments.

Sighing and muttering something about waiting and seeing, her mom pinned a section of hair up and out of the way and unrolled another section to examine. "All right, hold still."

"I am," said Bailey.

"No, you're not," said her mother. "You're wriggling."

Bailey could tell her mom was getting more and more grumpy about the nits and the nitpicking, not to mention the choir and the laundry and the house being a wreck. She tried to hold still. But the problem with sitting still was there was nothing to do except think. And all she could think about was Apollo and Olivia, all mixed up together.

Her bird was gone. He was gone because she'd been showing off for Olivia. Who was gone, too, in a way.

It took getting lice, and having the lousiest birthday, but Bailey got it now: She and Olivia weren't best friends anymore. And she got that she couldn't totally blame Olivia—not if she didn't want to be totally hypocritical. She got that maybe it was just as much her fault as Olivia's. She'd even gone over to Olivia's and said sorry!

But what good did that do? What was supposed to happen now? It was like looking at Olivia and her orange hair through the crisscross lines of the screen door. Everything was all fuzzy. It seemed like Olivia still wanted to be friends, just not *best*. But how were you supposed to be plain old friends with the person who used to be your best friend?

Thinking too much was definitely one problem with sitting still. The other problem was being a sitting duck.

"Don't forget," said Bailey's mom. "You still have those thank-you notes to write."

Thank-you notes was another thing her mom was a big believer in, along with honoring commitments and putting a positive spin on things. But why did her mom always remind her about stuff at a time when it was impossible for Bailey to do it?

"I know," said Bailey. "I'll do them."

After she'd opened Olivia's present, she'd gone ahead and opened the other gifts. There was a yo-yo from Tucker. A diary with a lock and key from Lexy. And a tiger-stripe bandanna from Arianna.

"They were nice," her mom went on. "Your friends. You should have them over again."

"Maybe," said Bailey. The last time they came out she'd lost her bird, which wasn't their fault, but it didn't make her in any rush to invite them again.

"Will they be at the middle school next year?"

Bailey felt the long tines of the special comb

being drawn over her scalp, and her hair pulled taut. "Probably," she answered. "I guess."

"You know," said her mom slowly.

Uh-oh. Here it came. Bailey didn't really want to hear whatever her mom was trying to get at, but she didn't have much choice. She was stuck on the stool.

"It was bound to happen sometime."

There was a moment of silence while Bailey *didn't* ask what was bound to happen sometime. The worst thing about any silence now was the emptiness. Before, if she and her mom weren't talking, Apollo filled in the quiet spaces. Now there were no more frantic feed-me chirps. No pay-attention-to-me cheeps. Just empty silence.

"You and Olivia," her mom went on. "Probably you would have drifted apart in middle school. That's what people do, honeybee. It just happened a little sooner, is all."

"We wouldn't have drifted!" objected Bailey. "She's been my best friend since"—Bailey was so mad she couldn't talk right—"since forever!"

"You *turned into* best friends," said her mom. "And that was great! I'm just saying, nothing is *always*. There was a *before* and maybe . . ." She paused.

Don't, thought Bailey. Don't put a positive spin on this. Do not.

Bailey's mom ran the comb through Bailey's hair. "Maybe it's okay if there's an *after*," she finished.

Bailey shook her head. No.

"Stop," said her mom.

"Stop what?" demanded Bailey. "You're the one who should stop!"

"I mean, stop shaking your head back and forth," instructed her mom, pulling the comb through again. "I can't see what I'm doing."

"How much longer?" asked Bailey. It was bad enough getting nitpicked for nits, without her mom picking apart her whole life, too. "Are you almost done?"

"No!" screamed her mom.

But it wasn't a *no* in answer to Bailey's question. It

was a *no* of horror. Her mom had pulled a real, live, crawling-around louse from Bailey's hair.

"That's it!" she said as she dropped the louse into a small bowl filled with the special louse-killing shampoo. "That hair has got to go!"

Bailey thought fast. Her mom was already on edge from all the laundry and extra cleaning. Finding an actual living louse had pushed her right over the edge. This called for some serious begging.

"Mom," she pleaded. "Can't we try something else? *Please*? Other kids have lice and get rid of them! Can't you find out what they did? Mom, please don't make me cut it! This is really important to me."

"Well, it's really important to me not to have vermin in our house!"

"Mom," she said, "you know why I'm growing it, remember?"

"Of course I do, but I don't think Aunt Jess would be in favor of vermin, either." Her mom paused and took a deep calming-down breath. Then another. "But I hear you. Okay. We can give it a little longer. We can . . . try something else."

She reached for the telephone and ended up having a long talk with Emma and Rosa's mom about alternative methods of lice eradication.

"What did she say?" asked Bailey when her mom put down the phone.

"She said the girls were really upset they couldn't come to your party," said Bailey's mom as she started rummaging through the refrigerator. "But they were dealing with lice, so it just didn't work. And she said what finally worked for them was the mayonnaise method."

Bailey didn't like the sound of that. "The mayonnaise method?"

The theory was that if there were any lice the mayonnaise smothered them, slowing them down so they couldn't move. Or breed. Or lay more eggs.

You still had to comb out the lice and pick out any old nits, but while you were doing that, the mayonnaise should stop the lice from making any *new* nits.

"Looks like we're out of mayonnaise," said Bailey's mom. She pulled out a jar and held it up. "All we seem to have is tartar sauce."

"Mom, no way! That's disgusting!"

"Agreed," said her mom. "But the main ingredient is mayonnaise."

"Mayonnaise and pickle relish!" said Bailey. "Can't we at least get some regular mayonnaise at the store?"

"Bailey Blecker," said her mother in a grim voice, "it is Sunday night. There is one store on this island, and it is closed. Now I know this is disgusting. So are lice. And no matter how much you love your aunt Jess, something has got to be done. Right now."

Bailey knew what any kid knows: When a grown-up says your last name, it's all over. To make it worse, her mom acted like it *wasn't* all over. She pretended Bailey had a choice.

"It's your choice," she said.

Why did grown-ups act like they were offering you a choice when they were really just threatening you? Letting your mom either cut your hair or dip your head in tartar sauce wasn't a choice!

Bailey's mom crisscrossed her arms. "Now are you going to get all stubborn on me?" she asked. "Or are we going to do this thing?"

CHAPTER 11

The Giant Fish Stick

The bell rang, lockers slammed, and kids hurried down the hall on their way to their classrooms.

Bailey was in no hurry. She planned on spending as long as possible trying to find a pencil in her locker. With her head as far *inside* her locker as she could get.

"Yo!" said a voice. "Avast there, Bailey! What's up?"

Bailey peeked out from her locker.

Tucker wore a buggy shirt, as usual—today's had a giant ladybug—and his new wardrobe staple, the blue bandanna. Which apparently made him feel the need to talk like a pirate whenever possible.

"Methinks 'tis fish sticks for lunch today!"

Bailey cringed. It wasn't fish sticks for lunch. It was her. Last night she had slept with her head gooped in tartar sauce, covered in a plastic shower cap. This morning she'd gotten up early to wash it out, but it still smelled. Make that, stank.

Max's head emerged from his locker. Bailey didn't know if the boys were just doing the pirate thing, like Tucker, or if it was lice prevention, but they were all wearing bandannas now, too. Max's was purple.

"Fish sticks?" he asked. "I love fish sticks!"

Emma opened her locker. "It's not fish sticks," she said. "I saw the menu."

Rosa closed her locker. "It's not," she agreed. "It's tacos today."

"Then *what*," demanded Lexy, "is that *awful* smell?"

Bailey wished they would all go away. "Who cares?" she snapped.

"What's the matter with you?" accused Lexy, sounding hurt.

"Nothing," said Bailey, her voice echoing inside her locker. "Just leave me alone, okay?"

"Blimey," said Tucker, "what's bugging you?"

What was bugging her? What *wasn't* bugging her was more like it. Bailey was mad. She was mad about her hair smelling like tartar sauce, just because she had lice. She was mad about having lice, just because somebody else in this school had them first and gave them to her. Why had she come to this stupid school in the first place, anyway? If she had stayed in the island school, maybe she would never have gotten lice. Maybe she would've stayed best friends with Olivia. And still have Apollo. And she knew that was all mixed up but that's how it felt—like everything bad was happening all at once. To her. And it was so unfair!

She came out from hiding in her locker and slammed the door shut. "That awful smell is me!" she blurted. "Okay? My mom's doing the mayonnaise method, except we were out of mayonnaise, so it's tartar sauce!" By now she was screaming. *"Okay?"*

"Not okay, Bailey!" said Mr. McGovern, who had suddenly appeared in the hallway.

He took a deep breath, and Bailey waited for him to find some way to turn a negative into a positive. He would probably say something like "We use our *inside* voices when we're inside."

Instead he said, "Bailey—I'd like you to spend recess with me today."

Indoor recess? Mr. M. made it sound like it was something good—spending recess with him—but Bailey wasn't stupid. She'd never had indoor recess before, but she knew what it meant. Indoor recess was a punishment.

She followed Mr. McGovern into the room, where he wrote her name on a corner of the whiteboard. The indoor recess corner. No big deal, Bailey told herself. Today might be a good day to miss outdoor recess, anyway. Outdoor recess could be brutal. That was when you would get teased for sure, if there was something to tease you for. Smelling like a giant fish stick, for example.

"Let's get busy, fifth graders," said Mr. McGovern. "We have lots to do today!"

The first thing on Mr. M.'s lots-to-do list was sharing from their Writer's Notebooks. They should pick the piece of writing they were most proud of to share with the class.

Tucker's hand shot up in the air. Mr. McGovern gave him the go-ahead nod, and Tucker went to the front of the room.

"Lice are a kind of parasite that live on the outside of a person. A tapeworm is a parasite that lives inside a person. In your guts! Tapeworms can get to be sixty feet long!"

He looked around, grinning, like everybody must be so happy to hear this fun fact about parasites.

Mr. McGovern asked, "Tucker, what source material did you use for this?"

"The Big Book of Parasites!" said Tucker. "My mom got it from the library!"

"Okay," sighed Mr. McGovern. "Go on."

"Cats and dogs can get worms, too. Once I saw my dog dragging its butt along the ground—"

"That's enough, Tucker!" said Mr. McGovern. "That is *not* appropriate."

But Tucker, inspired by David and Eli and Joey, who were cracking up, quickly added, "And I looked and saw a bunch of worms in his poop—" Tucker started laughing so hard himself that he couldn't finish his sentence.

Mr. McGovern rose and wrote Tucker's name on the indoor recess list, right below Bailey's.

Bailey started having second thoughts about indoor recess.

Mr. McGovern got the class back under control and asked for another volunteer. He studied the raised hands, like he was trying to find somebody who wouldn't read something too inappropriate.

Apparently he didn't like his choices, because finally he said the name of somebody whose hand wasn't raised.

"Arianna," he said, "will you read us something from your Writer's Notebook?"

Arianna went to the front of the room. She looked terrified. She gazed down at her notebook, then around the room. Her gaze stopped on Bailey.

Bailey had problems but being shy wasn't one of them. She tried to give Arianna an encouraging smile.

Arianna smiled back. "I wrote a poem," she announced.

"One mouse, many mice.

One louse, many lice.

Twice I had lice,

And it wasn't very nice."

Mr. McGovern clapped loudly. "Well done, Arianna! A poem!"

Emma gave a brief talk on their household. How first she had lice but Rosa didn't. Then she didn't but Rosa did. And then they both did. But now they didn't!

The Giant Fish Stick

Mr. McGovern was back to his positive self. He kept smiling and clapping and praising everybody's writing.

They heard from Rashad, who wrote about how glad she was that she didn't have lice. She said that once she had poison ivy and it was really itchy. And she knew that lice made you itchy. So she felt bad for the kids who had lice.

"Now that's what I call being empathetic!" said Mr. McGovern. He jumped up and pointed to the pair of flip-flops glued to the *Walking in Your Buddy's Shoes* empathy poster. "I think everyone would agree that Rashad has earned a sticker for our class."

The stickers weren't supposed to be a contest. No single kid was going to win if they got the most stickers. The empathy sticker chart was supposed to be cumulative, because when anybody was empathetic, everybody was a winner.

Mr. M. peeled off a sticker of a sneaker and put it on the class chart next to Rashad's name.

Bailey put her tartar-sauce-smelling, bandanna-covered head down on her desk. Was this ever going to end? Why did they have to keep studying lice anyway? Whatever happened to their unit on the American Revolution?

Lexy raised her arm—the one that wasn't in a sling. "How long do we have to keep studying bugs? I thought we were supposed to be studying the American Revolution?"

Bailey lifted up her tartar-sauce-smelling, bandanna-covered head. What was going on? Was Lexy becoming less irritating? Or was she becoming just as irritating as Lexy?

Mr. McGovern answered Lexy's spoken and Bailey's unspoken question.

"That's a very good question, Lexy. We did make a little excursion from the curriculum to study lice."

Mr. McGovern gave a minilecture to explain why it was okay that they were so far off topic. He said that lice were part of the natural world, and the students were part of a community. And that members of a community had to support each other. Respect each other. And show empathy for each other.

"But you're right," he finished. "We do need to get back to our study of the American Revolution. And we will, this afternoon. I've been working out the details of something really special. Now, I don't want to say anything else until the plan is finalized, but I hope to have some exciting news for you right after recess!"

The more Mr. McGovern talked, the more excited he got. And the more worried Bailey got. She had a bad feeling in her stomach, like she'd just eaten a brownie way too fast. This was a teacher who thought kids having lice was a teachable moment. If Mr. M.'s hopes were this far up, it couldn't be good.

CHAPTER 12

All Thanks to You, Bailey Blecker

After lunch, Bailey slowly walked along the *Walking in Your Buddy's Shoes* footsteps from the cafeteria to the classroom. Tucker was already there ahead of her, sitting with Arianna. She'd expected Tucker. But what was Arianna doing here?

"Bailey!" said Mr. McGovern. "Welcome. Listen, I know this whole lice thing has been supertough. So hang in there, okay? Now, take a seat with these guys. I'm going to make a phone call and eat my lunch."

He pulled a sandwich from a brown paper bag and picked up the phone.

That was it? That's all that happened when you had to stay in for recess? Mr. M. said *hang in there?*

Bailey sat down at the table with Tucker and Arianna.

"Hey," she said. "What are you doing here?"

"I was inappropriate," boasted Tucker.

"I know that," said Bailey. "I know why you're here. I meant Arianna."

"Mr. M. lets me stay in and read sometimes," explained Arianna.

Bailey realized that Arianna wasn't always on the playground at recess. She'd never thought about why, though. Now she thought that it probably wasn't easy for Arianna. It was bad enough, coming at the start of fifth grade and not being shy, like Bailey. But it would be even harder starting halfway through the year— especially if you always had your leopard-spotted head in a book, like Arianna.

But instead of reading now, Arianna ripped open a small bag of pretzels and offered them around. "Whatever happened—" She started to say something and then stopped, her face scrunched with worry. Her purple glasses were slipping down her nose, and she pushed them back where they belonged. "You know— with your bird?"

"Yeah, what's the story?" asked Tucker with his mouth full of pretzel. "Did you find him yet, matey?"

Bailey looked at Tucker. It was hard to take seriously a kid wearing a blue bandanna and a giant ladybug shirt, who talked like a pirate and who thought worms in his dog's poop was a good subject for an essay. But it seemed like he seriously wanted to know. And Arianna definitely seemed like she cared.

She nibbled a salty pretzel and shook her head. "No," she said. "Not yet."

"Really?" he asked. "That sucks! I lost my dog once—"

"No offense, Tucker," interrupted Arianna, "but

I really don't think Bailey wants to hear about your dog."

Tucker defended himself. "I wasn't going to talk about *that*! I'm just saying, I know how it feels. It feels, like, really bad."

"Thanks," said Bailey.

She didn't know what else to say, and for once Tucker didn't say anything else, either. Like he really did understand how bad she felt.

In the quiet, Bailey could hear the shouts of the kids out on the playground, and Mr. M. on the phone saying, "Yes . . . yes, absolutely! . . . Yes, that's outstanding!"

He hung up the phone.

"That was it!" he crowed. "That was the president of the Fox Island Historical Society. Our class has been invited to help reenact the Boston Tea Party!"

He took a giant breath, like he was saving the best news for last. "And it's all thanks to you, Bailey Blecker!"

Mr. M. was too excited to listen when Bailey tried

to explain that it wasn't really thanks to her. She hadn't wanted it to happen, and she hadn't tried to make it happen. But it was happening. When you put history-crazy Mr. Adams together with positive-thinking, lemons-into-lemonade Mr. McGovern, things happened.

Make that, things spun out of control.

That very afternoon, permission forms went home. *I* (name of parent or guardian) *give permission for my child* (name of child) *to take part in the Fox Island Historical Society Revolutionary War Reenactment Day, on Sunday, May 3. A bag lunch will be provided. Please, no open-toed shoes.* That was just one more crazy thing about this crazy plan—who ever heard of a field trip on a weekend? Bailey wondered how many kids would actually show up—only three had shown for her birthday—but Mr. M. said he was counting on one hundred percent participation.

On Tuesday, roles were assigned. Fifth graders would be playing the parts of the colonists, along with the Fox Island fifth graders. Mr. Adams and his cronies would play the parts of the British soldiers. Bailey was given a starring role—Samuel Adams—and a speech to memorize. She told Mr. M. that she didn't know if she could memorize such a long speech in such a short time, but Mr. M. said he was sure she could. He was counting on her. Bailey thought all Mr. M.'s counting might have a few errors in it.

Wednesday they started rehearsing. Bailey read the lines of her speech. It was all about how people shouldn't have to pay taxes to a government unless they had a say in the government—which the colonists didn't. And how there were three boats in Boston Harbor, full of tea. If the colonists didn't want to pay the tax on the tea, they couldn't let the tea come off the boats and into the town. They had to get rid of the tea.

On Thursday the nurse did a classroom-wide louse check. One by one, students were sent to the office to be checked. At the end of the day, Mr. M. reported the nurse's findings. He couldn't say which kids still had lice and which didn't. That was confidential. But he could say that far fewer kids had lice this week than last week! The louse infestation wasn't over, but it seemed to be slowing down. For the time being, however, it was *strongly suggested* that all students continue to take precautions to prevent the spread of lice. Not a problem, thought Bailey, as she looked around the room at the assortment of kerchiefs, scarves, hijabs, and bandannas. Not a single kid was bareheaded.

The next day, Friday, was the first of May. Waiting for the morning boat, Bailey checked the community bulletin board. Where was her "lost bird" notice? It was gone!

No, it wasn't. It was just covered up by somebody's offer to mow lawns. Bailey moved things around so her sign showed again, then walked down the gangplank onto the boat and climbed the stairs to the upper deck. As the horn sounded and the ferry pulled away, she looked back at the island. The trees weren't bare anymore. Their branches were completely hidden by their new leaves. Leaves the same bright, light green color as Apollo's wings.

Where *was* he? She had walked around and around the island without seeing a single sign of him. Was he perched in one of those big, leafy trees, camouflaged so she couldn't see him? Luckily the weather had been warm, and it was going to keep getting warmer. And there were bird feeders full of food and birdbaths full of fresh water, all over the island. He could be fine. She could still find him.

Unless she didn't.

Bailey pushed that thought out of her head. She couldn't not find him. She had to find him. Soon. Super-soon, because her mom had phoned Aunt Jess and spent a long time bragging about Bailey's starring role in Reenactment Day and Aunt Jess had said she wouldn't miss it for the world. On Sunday she was coming out to the island for the first time in weeks. Bailey felt like she was on a seesaw.

She was going to see Aunt Jess. Up!

But Aunt Jess was going to see that Apollo was gone. Down.

But—up!—Aunt Jess was going to see her in Reenactment Day!

But what if she blew her speech and looked like an idiot?

Quickly Bailey pulled a crumpled paper from her backpack and started madly trying to memorize . . . *the right to govern ourselves . . . the tea shall be sent back . . . no duty shall be paid . . .* but she was having trouble concentrating because her neck itched. She reached beneath her bandanna and scratched. Stupid lice! She was sick of lice! She tried to push the thought of them out of her head, too. Which was hard when the stupid things were *on* your head! She wondered which kids were on the nurse's louse-free list, and which were on the lousy list, with her.

"You may wish to cover your ears," warned the captain over the loudspeaker. "Brief blast of the horn."

The horn blasted, the ferry docked, and Bailey

stuffed her speech into her backpack and started heading up the gangplank toward the yellow bus waiting to take the older kids to their schools, and take her to Casco Elementary. It was the usual scramble. People going to the city streamed off the boat, and a crowd of people going to the island waited nearby, ready to stream on. There was a place where people piled up the stuff they would take with them to the island, once it was their turn to get on the boat—building materials and groceries and bicycles.

And a cage.

A cage?

A cage—a small, empty cage. A bird-size cage! A cage for a bird!

Who did that cage belong to? Bailey had to see. But she couldn't. She was right in the thick of the other kids as they surged toward the bus. Middle and high school kids who were bigger and taller than she was. The next thing she knew she was on the bus. She scurried to a seat and peered out the dirty window.

The cage was gone from the pile. Somebody had picked it up, but who?

As the bus started to pull away from the ferry terminal, Bailey scanned the crowd getting onto the boat.

There! She spotted the cage. But she couldn't tell who was carrying it because their face was facing away from her. All she got was a glimpse of the cage-carrier's head.

Circled by a green bandanna headband.

. . . .

CHAPTER 13

Operation Birdcage Search

A headband," said Bailey. "Made from a green bandanna."

It was recess, and kids were spread out all over the playground. Max was scaling the spiderweb. David, Eli, and Joey were kicking around a soccer ball. Rashad and Emma and Rosa were digging in the vegetable garden with the new teacher's aide.

Bailey was sitting on the stone steps of the amphitheater with Tucker, Lexy, and Arianna, telling them what she had seen that morning.

"Some guy wearing a green bandanna had an empty birdcage."

Lexy got it in a flash. "Which means maybe they have a bird to go in that cage! Maybe Green Bandanna Guy has Apollo!"

"Yo," said Tucker. "That is genius."

Bailey nodded. For once she didn't mind completely agreeing with Lexy. This news was too good. An empty cage needed a bird. A found bird needed a cage. The cage was for Apollo.

"Now what?" asked Arianna. "What are you going to do now?"

"Search every house!" cried Tucker. "Take no prisoners! We're pirates, aren't we?"

"Actually, no," said Lexy.

"I guess I'll just go door-to-door and knock," said Bailey. "And ask if anyone found a bird."

Arianna—the girl who had passed her times tables in third grade *and* knew enough to wear a louse-

146

prevention bandanna—asked a question that was scary-smart.

"What if they don't tell the truth? What if they want to keep Apollo?"

"I didn't think of that," admitted Bailey. "I just figured maybe somebody found a bird who never saw my 'lost bird' sign. But if they wanted to keep him . . . wow. I don't know."

"That wouldn't be right!" said Lexy. "That would be so totally wrong!"

"Maybe you don't tell them why you're there," said Tucker. "You just knock, and they come to the door, and if the bird is in there, you'll hear it, right?"

Bailey agreed that there was no way she *wouldn't* hear Apollo, who would start to cheep and chatter nonstop if he heard her voice.

"But you should have some reason for knocking on people's doors," suggested Arianna.

"Like selling stuff!" said Tucker.

"Like what?" asked Bailey. "What would I sell?"

Tucker said authentic pirate booty and everybody told him to stuff it and get real. Arianna thought friendship bracelets would be good, but Lexy pointed out that you were supposed to give friendship bracelets to friends, not sell them for money.

"Plus, I need something I can make fast," said Bailey. "Something everybody wants."

"I know! I know!" Lexy jumped up from the stone she was sitting on and started hopping up and down. "I know, I know, I know!"

"News flash," said Tucker. "Lexy knows the answer!"

Lexy didn't take time to bicker with Tucker. She just made a face at him and said, triumphantly, "Brownies!"

"Brownies are good," admitted Tucker.

Bailey grinned at Lexy. "Brownies are brilliant!"

Everyone agreed: Brownies could be made fast. Brownies were a good cover for a secret birdcage search.

Arianna spoke up. "But you should have some special reason for selling them," she said.

"Good idea," said Lexy. "You mean like a fund-raiser?"

"My mom's always baking stuff for church," said Bailey. "She says people will buy anything if it's for a good cause!"

"So what's a good cause?" asked Arianna.

They were quiet for a second, thinking. David, Eli, and Joey ran past, pretending to be angry American colonists.

"Tyranny!" they shouted. "Taxation without representation is tyranny!"

Bailey grinned as she figured out the perfect good cause for a secret birdcage-search brownie fund-raiser.

"The Historical Society," she said. "They always need money!"

The bell rang to mark the end of recess, and kids started streaming past them on their way into the building.

"Sounds like a plan," said Tucker. "So when do we do this thing?"

"Right away!" said Lexy. "Like, tomorrow!"

"Should we take that same boat we took last time?" asked Arianna. "In the morning? And then we can make brownies, and then help you sell them?"

More kids ran past, but Bailey was too surprised to move. She had thought they were just brainstorming about what *she* was going to do. She hadn't realized that Tucker, Lexy, and Arianna were all talking about doing it together.

Now the teacher's aide was herding stragglers off the playground. "Let's go!" she called.

Tucker and Lexy and Arianna didn't listen to the teacher's aide. They didn't go anywhere. They were waiting for Bailey to answer.

Bailey wasn't going anywhere, either, but it felt like her brain was. It felt like she was having a lightbulb moment *and* a birthday candle moment at the same time. Tucker and Lexy and Arianna wanted to help her. And she wanted their help. Because they were friends now.

"Let's go!" scolded the teacher's aide, and because she was new and didn't know everybody yet, she added the standard didn't-know-your-name word: "Come on, friends!"

Bailey grinned. "Thanks, friends," she said. "That'd be great."

And for the first time in a long time, Bailey felt like things really were going great.

She had a plan. She had friends who were coming the next morning, to help with the plan. And soon— really soon—she would have Apollo back.

The only problem was, she still had lice.

. . . .

CHAPTER 14

Pass the Brownies

The first door they knocked on, nobody answered. Even though Bailey was pretty sure somebody was home, because she could hear the television.

At the second house, a lady Bailey knew from church stood in the middle of her kitchen and called through the screen door that she couldn't buy any brownies today because she was on a strict diet.

At the third house, a little kid actually started yelling, "Mom! Mom! It's the kids in bandannas!" and the mom scolded, "Get away from the door, Morgan!"

"I'm selling brownies!" Bailey tried. "It's a fund-raiser!"

"Sorry," said the mom. "No thanks!"

Bailey would have liked to explain to the mom all the things she had learned about lice. That the lice couldn't fly or hop from her onto Morgan. They could only crawl. So as long as she didn't touch heads with the kid or share a hairbrush—or a bandanna—then Morgan and her mom were safe. But Morgan's mom had already closed the door.

It was the same everywhere they went. Nobody would let them in the door. Everybody seemed to know that Bailey had lice, and that any kids she was with might have lice, too. Nobody wanted the bandanna kids coming anywhere near them. Nobody bought a single brownie.

"What is up with this place?" asked Lexy. "How can everybody know you have lice?"

Bailey sighed. "It's an island thing," she said. "Everybody knows everything."

They had given up knocking on doors and were wandering down the road under a gray sky. The shaggy forsythia bushes had dropped all their yellow flowers on the ground, like when Apollo molted and dropped his yellow tail feathers on the floor of the aviary.

They walked past a little house with its name painted on a piece of driftwood—MY KOZY KOTTAGE—and a birdbath in the front yard. Bailey tried to think about Apollo finding water in birdbaths and seeds in bird feeders. She tried not to think about cats. And hawks. And rain. And Aunt Jess, who was coming tomorrow, and who still didn't know. How was she supposed to tell Jess that she'd lost Apollo?

"And what's with all the houses having names?" asked Tucker. He read the names of the houses they passed. *"Paradise Found. Morning Glory. Billy's Place.* Why would anybody name a house?"

"It's an island thing, too," said Bailey.

"Weird," declared Tucker. "So what do we do now?"

"I don't know," said Bailey. She had no idea where

to go or what to do. The only thing she wanted now was impossible: She wished she could go back in time. Have a do-over. Never open the cage door.

"How about the beach?" suggested Arianna. "Should we look there?"

Bailey didn't think Apollo would be in such an open, windy place. But going to the beach was better than standing here, doing nothing.

"Sure," she said. "Good idea."

It was such a looks-like-rain day that Driftwood Beach was deserted, except for an old man pacing up and down with his metal detector. And except for the birds. Little sandpipers scooted up and down the sand as the waves washed in and out, and up above, seagulls zigged and zagged across the cloudy sky. Bailey and the others took off their shoes, rolled up their pant legs, and walked along the tide line, staying just out of reach of where the waves splash-landed on the sand.

"People are so stupid!" said Bailey. "Don't they

know they won't get lice by letting us talk to them for five minutes? What are we supposed to do now?"

"Eat the brownies ourselves?" suggested Tucker.

"Be serious!" scolded Lexy. "We're not talking about eating. We need another plan."

"We had a good plan!" objected Bailey.

She had been so sure it was a great plan. And the beginning of the plan had gone great. They had made a ton of brownies. And it was so easy to imagine the end of the plan: Apollo back in the aviary. She just hadn't figured on the middle part bombing so badly. Because of lice.

"Except we forgot that people think lice are gross and disgusting," said Tucker.

"Don't forget itchy," added Lexy.

"And itchy," agreed Bailey, and then wished she hadn't. Just *saying* the word itchy made her *feel* itchy. She stopped walking, reached under her bandanna, and scratched savagely until the nape of her neck was burning hot. While she stood there at the water's edge an extra-big wave surged in, but she didn't run for higher ground. She let the cold water rush around her ankles, and as the water drew back out to sea, she felt her feet sink into the wet sand.

"Cold!" declared Tucker.

"No kidding," said Lexy. "What did you expect?"

"Stop, you guys," said Arianna. "Don't change the subject."

"What's the subject?" asked Tucker.

Lexy groaned. "Apollo?" she asked in an accusing voice. "Bailey's bird? The whole reason we're here?"

"I knew that," said Tucker.

"Listen," said Arianna. "I have an idea. What if we found somebody to help? Somebody who doesn't wear a bandanna."

"Blimey!" said Tucker. "I could take mine off!"

"You've got a buzz cut," reminded Lexy. "Same difference. People see a buzz cut and they think, lice."

"I don't mean you," said Arianna. "I mean somebody who isn't in our class."

"Like who?" asked Tucker.

"Bailey's friend. The one who came over on her birthday."

Another wave landed on the beach and then slipped back out to sea, and Bailey's feet sank a little deeper in the sand.

"Olivia," she said. "I don't think so."

"Why not?" asked Lexy. "Isn't she, like, your best friend? You always used to talk about her in the beginning of the year."

"She's not my best friend anymore," said Bailey.

"Since when?" pressed Lexy.

"I don't know!" cried Bailey. Even though she did know. At least, she knew when "anymore" *started* being true: when she started at Casco Elementary. Then what? It wasn't like they had a big fight or anything. It was more like they had just drifted apart, like her mom said, because they *were* apart.

Another wave came and went, and Bailey's feet sank even deeper. She used to do this all the time with Olivia. They would stand on the waterline and let their feet sink deeper and deeper. First just their toes were covered in sand. Then their whole feet. Then their ankles. The longer they stood there, the deeper they sank. The more stuck they got.

But that was pretend stuck. All you had to do to get unstuck was lift up your feet. Easy.

But it wasn't that easy to get unstuck in real life. In real life, Bailey still wanted to be best friends. Not *former* best friends. And she didn't want to ask for help from her former best friend.

"I just don't want to ask her, okay?"

There was an awkward, silent moment, and then an extrabig wave rolled in. Everybody shouted and unsquelched their feet and scrambled to higher ground. They ran up to the dry sand and plopped down in the spot where they'd left their shoes and the brownies.

"Permission to eat the brownies now, Captain?" asked Tucker.

Bailey was not in the mood to play pirate. But these guys had been really nice, and if Tucker wanted to play pirate and eat brownies, maybe she should go along.

"Whatever," said Bailey. "But I'm not your captain."

"Blimey!" said Tucker. "I'm the captain and you're me best matey!"

"Blimey," echoed Bailey. "Now pass the brownies."

CHAPTER 15

Teatime

It had rained during the night, and in the morning all the trees and bushes and flowers were steaming in the sun. Everything felt washed and clean. It was going to be a beautiful spring day for the Fox Island Historical Society's reenactment of the Boston Tea Party. Bailey was sitting on the porch with her mom. Her mom had a cup of coffee and Bailey had a glass of lemonade.

The breeze picked up, and somebody's wind chimes began chiming. A robin hopped across the grass. Bailey's head started hopping with questions.

Where did the robin go when it rained? It had a nest, right? But Apollo didn't have a nest. Had he been outside in the rain? Or had he been sheltered by the person with the cage? But if somebody had found Apollo, why didn't they call her? And how was she supposed to find them if nobody would let her in the door because she had lice?

Bailey sipped her lemonade. She couldn't believe how complicated her lousy life was getting! Lice were lousing up all her plans. She wanted to keep growing her hair for *Care Through Hair*, and she wanted to find Apollo, too. But after yesterday's failed brownie bird-cage search, she wasn't sure she could do both. This was one time it seemed like being stubborn was *not* going in her favor. What if she couldn't be stubborn about both her hair and Apollo? What if she had to choose?

"How long since Apollo escaped?" she asked her mom.

Her mom took a sip of coffee. "Two weeks."

"How long since I got lice?"

"Three weeks," said her mom. She rested her hand on Bailey's kerchief-covered head. "It won't be forever, honeybee. We're making progress—sort of."

Since the tartar-sauce treatment, Bailey's mom hadn't found any more live lice, but she was still picking nits out, day by day.

Bailey looked at her mom in surprise. "I thought you wanted me to cut my hair?"

Her mom shrugged—another surprise. Her mom didn't usually give a *whatever* shrug.

"I do think we'd be rid of the lice sooner with shorter hair," she said. "But if you're willing to tough it out, so am I."

"I thought you thought I was being too stubborn?"

Her mom didn't answer right away. She took another sip of coffee, then said, "I know I freaked, before, but I'm not freaked out now. I know how important this goal is to you. And it means a lot to me to see how—determined—you're being, for Aunt Jess's sake."

She reached under her chair. "I got you something," she said. She handed Bailey a brand-new bandanna. It had swirly red and blue stripes, with white stars. "For the big day!" she said. "Do you like it?"

Bailey would have liked the bandanna more if she didn't have to put it on her head and look like some kind of crazy, mixed-up flag. But she did like the feeling that for once her mom didn't think she was being too stubborn.

"I love it," she said. "Thanks, Mom."

She took off her red bandanna and tied on the swirly starry one, and then it was time to go meet the boat.

The entire population of the island seemed to have come out to meet the boat, too. The wharf was mobbed, and when the ferry docked, it got even more crowded. Here came what looked like the whole fifth-grade class of Casco Elementary, and their families, with a beaming Mr. McGovern. And dozens of people Bailey had never seen before paraded off in colonial garb, the women in long skirts and bonnets and the men in breeches. They must be the guests Mr. Adams had invited from the other historical societies all over New England.

Bailey scanned the crowd for Aunt Jess. Was that her? She felt her heart light up and fall at the same time, like a shooting star. It *was* Aunt Jess!—with her bare head covered by a white scarf.

Then suddenly Aunt Jess was there. First she hugged Bailey, then Bailey's mom, and then one more hug for Bailey before she patted her on the head.

"What's up?" she asked. "You bald under there, too?"

Bailey grinned. Aunt Jess was still Aunt Jess. And her white scarf was dotted with yellow bananas and green grapes and red strawberries.

"No," she said. "It's a long story."

Bailey's mom interrupted. "Well, no time for long stories now. Look, there's your teacher heading up to the Historical Society. You better scoot, honeybee. We'll be watching!"

Gratefully, Bailey scooted. Her mom had not only saved her from explaining about the bandanna, she had saved Bailey from the story that she *really* didn't want to tell. The one where she lost Apollo. She would tell Aunt Jess everything, but not now. Now it was time for the Tea Party.

The lawn of the Historical Society was just as crowded as the wharf. The guests from other historical societies had made their way here and were wandering around in their colonial clothes. Most of them seemed to be old men with Mr. Adams–style curlicue mustaches, but there were a few women and kids, too. Dogs on leashes barked and seagulls wheeled overhead, squawking. Even the flower beds hummed with bees dipping in and out of big pink tulips.

Bailey came up to where Arianna, Lexy, and Tucker were standing on the grass. Around them swirled David and Eli and Joey, Rashad and Emma and Rosa, Max and all the other kids from their class. Across the lawn were the Fox Island fifth-grade boys,

Aidan and Hayden and Sam. And there—not like Bailey was *looking*, but it was impossible *not* to see—was the bright frizz of orange hair, pulled back in a ponytail. Olivia, standing by herself.

"Young colonists!" called Mr. Adams, waving the fifth graders over to a big tree.

"This tree," he announced, with a crazed look on his face, "represents the Liberty Tree, an *actual tree* where the colonists had their meeting."

Mr. Adams started going over their instructions. Bailey would give her speech, and others would say their lines. Then there was going to be an exciting addition to the event! Just as the real colonists had stormed a wharf, they were going to run down to the actual wharf. On the north side of it was a ramp leading down to a float. Tied up to the float they would find a small sailboat. In the sailboat were some boxes full of dried seaweed that was supposed to look like tea, that they were supposed to dump into the water.

Bailey was thinking that a lot of things were

supposed to happen without ever having been rehearsed, but there was no time for questions. On went Mr. Adams. As they knew from their studies, the colonists had disguised themselves so the British soldiers wouldn't recognize them. They'd put chimney soot on their faces and wrapped themselves in blankets, pretending to be Mohawk Indians. He looked doubtfully at the heads of the Casco Elementary kids.

"The bandannas," he asked. "Must they be worn at all times?"

Bailey looked at Tucker's blue bandanna and Arianna's leopard kerchief and Rashad's sparkly scarf. She had gotten so used to everybody's head being covered, she'd forgotten how unusual they must seem to other people.

"It was sort of a rule," said Bailey. "Because of the—lice."

Mr. McGovern spoke up. "Actually," he explained, "our school made a *suggestion*, but it's not a rule. As far as the school is concerned, students are free to uncover their heads—if it's okay with their moms and dads."

Everybody started talking about whether they should—or should not—take off their bandannas. Whether they did—or did not—have lice. Bailey had wondered who had gotten a clean bill of health at the last head check. Now she had to know for sure. She asked one kid after another and got their answers: no; not me; not anymore. The answers all pointed to the same thing. A few kids had been lucky never to have lice. Other kids had suffered through them and gotten rid of them. But apparently when Mr. M. reported that the nurse had found lice on "far fewer kids," he was covering for the one and only kid who still had them. Bailey Blecker.

"Young historians!" cried Mr. Adams. "Can we please get organized?"

Mr. Adams sounded a little frazzled, and Bailey felt sorry for him. She felt sorry for the spectators, too. They were going to watch a bunch of kids pretending to be colonists, pretending to be Mohawk Indians. In bandannas. She didn't think anybody had that good of an imagination.

She raised her hand. "I have an idea," she said. "I could keep my bandanna on, since I still have—lice. Then everybody else could take theirs off, and they'd still be safe, right? 'Cause I don't see why everybody should have to wear one, just because of me."

Mr. M. took a big breath, considering her idea. With his cheeks full of air he looked like the picture of Old Brother West Wind in the book of nursery rhymes Bailey used to read. "What does everyone else think of Bailey's idea?"

Bailey took a deep breath, too. Lilacs made the air smell sweet. What *would* everyone think of her idea? She saw Arianna and Lexy and Tucker huddled together, whispering.

Raising her hand, Arianna stepped forward. "Mr. M.? I don't think it's fair to let Bailey decide what we should all do."

"That's like the King of England trying to boss around the colonists," Lexy pointed out. "But Bailey's not the boss of us."

For a second Bailey was too surprised to speak. She wasn't trying to boss anybody around! She was just trying to be nice! But when she tried to explain she didn't get any further than "That's not what I meant"—before Arianna caught her eye. Through her purple-rimmed glasses she gave Bailey a look that clearly said, *I got this*.

Tucker piped up, "Why should she get to take away my right to dress up like a pirate? Isn't that, like, one of my Constitutional rights?"

"The rights outlined in the Constitution are somewhat broader," began Mr. Adams. "You have your Freedom of Expression, perhaps."

Arianna spoke up again. "I think we should take a vote," she declared. "So everybody can help decide what we do. Because maybe everybody *wants* to express themselves through their ... uh ... heads. With Bailey."

Tucker added, "Isn't that the whole point of this Tea Party thing? Because the colonists wanted to govern themselves?"

Mr. McGovern looked like he wanted to hug Tucker. "Good connection, Tucker," he said.

"A vote!" cried Mr. Adams, beaming. "By all means, let the people be heard!"

Somebody shouted "Vote!" and David and Eli and Joey took up the chant, "Vote! Vote! Vote!"

Mr. M. asked, "All those in favor of Bailey's idea?"

Nobody raised their hand. Nobody was voting to let her be the only one in a bandanna, even though she was the only one left with lice.

"All those opposed?"

Bailey looked around. Every hand was raised. Somehow Tucker and Lexy and Arianna had convinced everybody that a vote to wear bandannas was a vote for freedom. And now everybody in her class was voting to look just as silly as she would, pretending to be a colonist pretending to be an Indian. In a bandanna.

"The people have spoken," said Mr. Adams. "You will be bandanna-wearing colonists!"

Bailey turned to Arianna and Lexy and Tucker. "You guys," she said. "I wasn't trying to boss anybody around."

"We *know* that," said Lexy. "We're not stupid."

"Besides, we look so good in our bandannas," boasted Tucker. "Especially me."

"We just figured you shouldn't be the only one," explained Arianna. "'Cause I know how that feels."

Bailey grinned. "Now that's what I call being empathetic!" she said in her best Mr. McGovern imitation. "I think you deserve a sticker of some sneakers."

"Any time," said Arianna, grinning back at Bailey.

"It *is* time," cried Mr. Adams. "Let the Tea Party begin!"

CHAPTER 16

Connect the Dots

Teatime meant speech time. Bailey stood on a wooden box, her heart ticking against her chest. Everyone was looking at her. She remembered the day in the library when all the kids were looking down at her on the beanbag like she had cooties, because she had lice. Now everyone was looking up at her on the box. She might still have lice but she didn't have *cooties*. She was Samuel Adams. She took a big gulp of lilac-filled air and recited her speech, ending on the solemn note, "This meeting can do nothing more to save the country."

She had done it! There was no time to celebrate, though, because Max delivered his line, "Taxation without representation is tyranny!" and David and Eli and Joey, and Sam and Aidan and Hayden, all whooped "Tyranny! Tyranny!"

Rashad declared, "Tonight the Boston Harbor is a teapot!"

Olivia had the last line, "To the wharf! To the wharf!" and suddenly Bailey found herself at the front of a mob of kids pretending to be a mob of angry colonists.

They were supposed to march. So she marched.

She marched along Little Loop and turned down Wharf Street. There were so many kids and reenactors and islanders and tourists marching along with her that Bailey could hardly tell who was the audience and who were the actors. But somewhere in the crowd, she knew, Aunt Jess and her mom were watching.

When she got to the wharf she marched past the spot where the ferry docked, way out to the end, where a long ramp angled down to a float on the water. The wharf on its pilings was always the same solid height, but the float floated up and down with the tide. The tide was low right now, so the float looked really far away. But she was supposed to go, so she went—down the ramp, which rocked back and forth as she clambered down, like the sort of amusement park ride that tried to shake you off.

At the bottom of the ramp she stepped onto the float, which bobbed wildly as more kids jumped on, like another ride. It wasn't bad if you didn't mind the feeling of bouncing around in a small, crowded space, with a cold ocean on every side if you fell in.

There was a small sailboat tied up to the float, just like Mr. Adams had promised. Bailey figured the boat couldn't be any tippier than the ramp or the float, so she hopped in, picked up one of the crates, and started flinging strands of dried seaweed into the water.

"No taxation without representation!" she shouted, getting into the spirit of things, and after emptying a box of seaweed tea she looked around to make sure she was doing it right. Which is when she realized that even if *she* was doing the right thing, some other things were going a little bit wrong.

Half a dozen colonist kids had basically gotten through the supposed-to list. They had made it either into the boat or at least onto the float. But most of the kids were on the ramp, stuck in what looked like a big traffic jam of Revolutionary War reenactors, who had joined the fifth graders. Some people looked like they were frozen with fear. They weren't moving. Some were still trying to get down to where the action was, and others were trying to go the other way, back up to safety. The moving people were having trouble getting past the frozen-with-fear people. To make matters worse, there were so many people on the float that it wasn't just bobbing. It was rocking wildly. Shouts of *Careful! Careful!* rang out.

It was chaos. But even with all the craziness, something stood out clearly. It was her friends. All of them. The ones who had asked for an election, and the ones who had voted to keep her company. Their heads were like the dots in a connect-the-dot puzzle.

On the float was a kid in a blue bandanna. Tucker, of course, always at the center of any action. The leopard-print bandanna was Arianna, naturally. She was at the foot of the ramp. Then came Max in a purple bandanna, just below Emma and Rosa in pink. A yellow kerchief halfway up was Lexy, looking like she couldn't decide whether it was better to go up or down. Behind her were David and Eli and Joey in matching army camouflage bandannas. And at the top of the ramp a tan hijab with silver sparkles was Rashad.

Beyond them was another fifth grader who hadn't made it onto the ramp. Way up on the wharf, twenty feet above, stood impossible-to-miss orange-haired Olivia.

And she was standing right next to a guy with a green bandanna headband circling his head.

"Tucker!" shouted Bailey, and pointed. "Look!"

"Shiver me timbers," said Tucker. "It's Bandanna Man!"

"I've gotta talk to him!" she said.

"Like how?" he asked. "Did you notice the crazy mob in between you and him?"

"Olivia's right next to him," she said. "She could stall him till I get there."

"Good luck with that," said Tucker. "First you gotta get the message to her."

Tucker was right. She called to the next closest kid who knew the whole story about Apollo and the Green Bandanna Guy.

"Arianna!"

Arianna looked over from the bottom of the ramp.

"The man who had the cage," yelled Bailey. "Up there. Next to Olivia."

"What?" called Arianna. She looked a little seasick.

Bailey tried again. It was sort of like the telephone game. Only it wasn't a game, and it wasn't working. Now Arianna looked seasick *and* confused.

"Do it like charades," said Tucker.

"The man in the green bandanna," shouted Bailey. "Who maybe has Apollo!" She pointed to her own bandanna and then made a circle around her head—meaning, *the bandanna headband*. Then she made little bird flaps with her hands.

Arianna's face lost its confused look. She got it. "Where?"

Bailey pointed up to where Olivia was. She saw Arianna nod and turn, and heard her call to Lexy, midway up the ramp. With shouts and gestures, Arianna passed Bailey's message on to Lexy.

By now Bailey had managed to climb out of the boat and get onto the float. The message was on its way, and she was right behind. But she was having trouble getting onto the ramp because an old geezer reenactor was blocking the way with one hand clamped in terror to each handrail. The reenactor was frozen, and she was stuck.

Looking up, she saw Lexy gesturing to Olivia. Who

looked down at Bailey. Had she figured out the two clues? She made a question mark face, her eyebrows raised as high as they would go, and pointed to the man standing next to her. *This guy? Apollo?*

Yesterday Bailey had refused to even think about asking Olivia for help. But if she wanted Apollo back, she needed her help now. It was time to get unstuck—fast. She nodded—*yes*—to Olivia's question, then put her hand flat on her heart and circled it. *Please.*

Quickly Olivia turned to the man and started talking to him—stalling him until Bailey could get there.

But Bailey wasn't watching anymore, because she was busy ducking under the arm of the frozen guy and plowing through the rest of the crowd. "'Scuse me," she said. "Coming through, 'scuse me."

Tucker tried to help by shouting, "The British are coming! Out of the way!"

"We are *not* the British," corrected Lexy.

"Never mind," said Arianna. "Just go!"

Bailey got to the top of the ramp with Tucker, Arianna, and Lexy in a jumble all around her. She stepped onto the wharf.

"This is Fred Fowler," announced Olivia, grinning. "And he knows where Apollo is!"

Bailey's head was spinning. She felt like she'd just stepped off a crazy American Revolution time-warp rocking-dock amusement park ride. Mr. Fowler—who looked like a country singer that Bailey's mom liked, with long, gray hair pulled back into a braid beneath the green headband—started explaining. He didn't live on the island, but his sister did. Except right now she was away and he was house-sitting. He had found Apollo on the screen porch of the house (there was a tear in the screen and maybe the bird got in that way) and got a cage to take care of the little guy for the time being, until he found its rightful owner.

He asked Bailey, "That'd be you, I take it?"

Head still spinning, she nodded. "Yes," she said.

She turned to Olivia. "Thanks."

Olivia grinned. "What are friends for?"

She didn't say best friends, but suddenly, just plain friends felt pretty good. Just plain friends felt great.

After that, things kept happening crazy dizzy fast. Mr. Fowler said he could take Bailey to his sister's house right now. Tucker and Lexy and Arianna wanted to go, too, and Mr. McGovern said it was okay if she got them back in time for the three o'clock boat and if one of their parents or another adult they knew went with them. Aunt Jess pushed through the crowd.

"Jessica Blecker," she said, shaking hands with Mr. McGovern. "Available as chaperone. Your mom's already back at the Historical Society," she explained to Bailey. "Apparently she volunteered to help with the luncheon. So where are we going?"

Ten minutes later, Fred Fowler stopped in front of a house with two signs: a business sign that read DOG DAY CARE, DOG BOARDING, DOG GROOMING; and a piece of driftwood painted with the house's name, PAWS AWHILE.

CHAPTER 17

Stepping Up

ailey sat beside Apollo's cage. The downstairs of the house seemed to be one big room—kitchen and living room and everything room—with a lot of dog beds scattered on the floor. And dogs on the dog beds. And seashells everywhere. It looked like the dog lady was one of those people that couldn't stop bringing things home from the beach, because every windowsill was lined with seashells.

Fred Fowler kept saying how sorry he was that he hadn't seen the "lost bird" sign, and Bailey kept saying it was okay. He wanted to hear how Bailey had known about him and the cage, and Tucker and Lexy and Arianna explained all about the failed brownie birdcage search. He laughed a big-belly bark of a laugh, and Aunt Jess laughed and shook her fruit-spotted head.

"Let me get this straight," she said. "You got lice. You lost Apollo. And you *never* called me?"

"I didn't want to bother you," said Bailey.

"Since when have you ever bothered me?" demanded Aunt Jess.

"Okay," admitted Bailey. "The reason I didn't tell you about the lice is . . . it's gross, right? And the reason I didn't tell you about Apollo is because I didn't want you to know he was lost until I found him."

"Well, you did good on that," said Aunt Jess. "Since I found out he was found before I knew he was lost."

Olivia sat next to Bailey and Apollo, not saying much, but listening and laughing, too.

Bailey decided that the whole thing with Olivia had been like the time she lost her favorite hoodie. She had lots of other jackets and sweatshirts, but none of them were her favorite. It wasn't until months later, when her mom had made those messy-room grumbling noises and made Bailey clean her bedroom down to the bare floors, including way underneath the bed, that Bailey had found the hoodie. Only, it had been lost so long it didn't fit right anymore. Her mom wanted to hand it down to somebody, but Bailey wouldn't let her. Even if she couldn't wear the hoodie, it was too special to throw away.

Bailey figured that being friends with Olivia again was going to be something like that. They'd been best friends for a long time. Then that got lost, and by the time Bailey found her again, the words "best friends" didn't exactly fit anymore. But that was okay. Now they were old friends.

And she had some pretty cool new friends. Lexy might still be a bit of a know-it-all, but she knew how to be a friend, too. Tucker was more than a bug-obsessed, pirate-pretending boy; he was a buddy. And quiet Arianna had spoken up, big-time, for Bailey's sake.

That was more than what a friend might do. That was something your maybe-new-best friend would do.

On top of Lexy and Tucker and Arianna were all the kids from Mr. M.'s class who had voted unanimously not to let her be the only colonist in a bandanna. Bailey decided they should *all* get *Walking in Your Buddy's Shoes* empathy stickers. Not for a joke. For real. Maybe tomorrow at school she would ask Mr. M. if everybody could have one.

Or maybe there was something else she could do for her friends. Like make sure their classroom was free from vermin.

"Mr. Fowler," she said. "Your sister grooms dogs, right?"

Fred Fowler nodded.

"So she has scissors?"

"Scissors, clippers, you name it, she's got it," he said. "Why?"

The thing about being stubborn was, you knew where you stood. You knew what you were wearing